She closed her eyes and inhaled deeply. "So this really was a marriage of convenience?"

"Caiti," he said roughly, "how 'convenient' does it feel when you're in my arms, in my bed?"

She shot up off the bench. "But would you have asked me to *marry* you if all this hadn't happened? Would you have slept with me in the first place if you'd known I was a virgin?"

That nerve flickered in his jaw again. "Probably not but—"

"Then that's what it is," she insisted. "You suddenly found yourself lumbered with an ex-virgin and a whole lot of awkward baggage at home—and do you know what?" Her eyes widened as it hit her. "I don't think you actually want to be in love with me or anyone, Rob Leicester."

Lindsay Armstrong was born in South Africa but now lives in Australia with her New Zealand-born husband and their five children. They have lived in nearly every state of Australia and have tried their hand at some unusual, for them, occupations, such as farming and horse-training—all grist to the mill for a writer! Lindsay started writing romances when their youngest child began school and she was left feeling at a loose end. She is still doing it and loving it.

Lindsay Armstrong

A BRIDE FOR HIS CONVENIENCE

HARLEQUIN®

TORONTO • NEW YORK • LONDON
AMSTERDAM • PARIS • SYDNEY • HAMBURG
STOCKHOLM • ATHENS • TOKYO • MILAN • MADRID
PRAGUE • WARSAW • BUDAPEST • AUCKLAND

ISBN 0-373-18848-X

A BRIDE FOR HIS CONVENIENCE

First North American Publication 2005.

CHAPTER ONE

FLYING into Cairns on a clear day was like floating into a wonderland.

Caiti Galloway watched, mesmerised, from her window seat as the jet descended over the Coral Sea. Brilliant turquoise and sandy patches studded the deep blue surface of the water where coral reefs rose from the depths like delicately tinted birds' eggs.

Although it was the gateway to her hometown of Port Douglas, it never failed to fascinate her.

Then they crossed the coastline and the flat patchwork of sugar-cane fields spread beneath them, flanked by darker green mountains that encroached on the city.

But as the wheels of the aeroplane touched down, she closed her eyes. Flying into Cairns might be magical but it was also a region that held many memories for her. Memories of falling in love with a man who wanted her but didn't love her.

She opened her eyes as the jet roared into reverse and started to slow down, and the woman sitting beside her smiled at her in relief.

There was the usual wait as they taxied to the terminal, the usual awkward scrambling for bags from the overhead lockers, but finally the passengers were

released into the tropical humidity of far-north
Queensland.

Being May, it wasn't as humid as it could be in
mid-summer, when it was like walking into a warm
blanket of air. Caiti had started her journey in much
cooler Canberra and now she felt overdressed in
jeans and a long-sleeved blouse.

Once in the terminal, she followed the signs to the
baggage carousel and at the same time looked about
for her cousin, Marion, who was coming to meet her.
Marion was the kind of person who always favoured
being early rather than late.

Indeed, her cousin was the reason Caiti was back
in Cairns. Marion was getting married in a fortnight
and Caiti was to be her chief bridesmaid.

There was no sign of her cousin yet and Caiti
frowned as she turned her attention to the carousel.
Preoccupied with her task, Caiti was unaware of the
tall man who, in the act of walking past, had stopped
abruptly and was studying her intently.

Rob Leicester would always stand out in a crowd
for his height alone but it didn't stop there. He was
dark-haired, broad-shouldered and tanned. Wearing
jeans and a khaki shirt, he looked all tough man. If
you looked closer, however, and many women did,
there was a latent sensuality about him that set them
wondering.

Did it come from those slightly moody hazel eyes?
A rather hard mouth? His lean, strong hands?

The two girls in their late teens he'd stopped beside were eyeing him with definite awe—as if precisely these thoughts were running through their minds.

Not that he even noticed them as he watched Caiti Galloway retrieve her luggage.

She hadn't changed. Still the same long, blue-black hair that had always reminded him of rough silk and fish-plaited today. The same smooth, golden skin—his fingers tingled as if he were touching her body. Still slender and essentially chic even in jeans, a plain white blouse and hiking boots.

How did she do it? he found himself wondering. Was it the little touches like the way her collar was turned up? Or the unusual leather belt that emphasised her narrow waist? She could even turn hiking boots into a fashion statement.

She pulled a bag off the carousel and turned fully towards him. Rob found himself holding his breath, wondering at what he would see in her long-lashed lavender-blue eyes when she recognised him.

It took a few moments as people moved about then the space between them cleared and she was looking straight at him, and, heaven help him, he thought grimly, her reaction couldn't have been more satisfactory.

Her eyes widened incredulously, she went paper pale then a rush of colour charged into her cheeks. She dropped her bag and her breasts, which he happened to have an intimate knowledge of, heaved beneath the white cotton of her blouse.

So, eighteen months apart hasn't lessened the impact I always used to have on you, Ms Galloway, was his immediate reaction as he moved forward smoothly and retrieved her bag.

'Caiti,' he murmured, 'this is a surprise. Have you decided to come back to me?'

Caiti swallowed several times and put her hand to her heart. 'R-Rob,' she stammered. 'What are you doing here? I was expecting my cousin, Marion…' She ran out of words and the flood of colour left her cheeks so that she was unnaturally pale again.

'You need a drink.' He took her elbow and began to steer her towards the bar.

'No… I mean…' she started to protest.

He said quietly, 'Don't be silly. You look as if you might faint.'

He found them a table in a secluded corner behind a potted palm and settled her in a chair then walked over the colourful carpet to the bar to order.

Caiti watched him with a hand to her throat and the utmost turmoil in her heart. Eighteen long months ago she'd run away from Rob Leicester because she'd fallen deeply in love with him, only to discover that she'd completely misread his feelings for her. It had been an agonising realisation and had plunged her into despair and desolation.

How could she have allowed herself to be swept off her feet so completely by this man? she'd asked herself repeatedly. Why was it only in hindsight that she could identify all the little signs along the way that had pointed to a man who wanted her but had no intention of allowing himself to fall in love with her?

By the greatest effort of will she'd pulled herself out of the chasm and put it all behind her. She'd even accepted Marion's invitation to come back to Cairns to be her bridesmaid, but now, as she stared across at Rob Leicester, her stunned reaction told her that she'd put nothing behind her.

All she'd done was paper over it in the most flimsy way because one glimpse of him had sent her reeling.

He turned towards their table with two glasses but someone tapped him on the arm, a man in his fifties. Rob put the glasses back on the bar to shake his hand and greet him. They chatted for a few moments and the other man said something to make Rob laugh— and Caiti caught her breath.

There were times when you couldn't doubt Rob Leicester was a tough, complicated man. There were other times, if you knew him well enough or thought you did, when he had a laid-back side to him that had enchanted her. Seeing him laugh, even only briefly, brought that side of him back to her in the most treacherous manner.

Her pulses started to hammer as her memories of him making love to her came flooding back in the most disturbing and intimate way. A tide of heat ran through her and the barren months were swept away as if he were actually kissing and caressing her body and she was writhing beneath the sweet torment of it.

He put two glasses of brandy on the table and pulled out his chair.

'W-who was that?' she asked disjointedly, anything to cover her disarray.

'A friend of my father's. Here,' he pushed a glass towards her, 'you certainly look as if you could do with it.'

She sipped some brandy gratefully, and coughed—it was neat, and made her eyes water but it helped.

'Sorry,' she said. 'I guess it was a bit of a shock, running into you like that.' She wiped her eyes with the back of her hand.

He sat back and studied her. 'I would have thought this part of the world would be a place to avoid if you didn't want to run into me, Caiti.'

'I'm only here for Marion's wedding.' She paused and thought back swiftly. 'I don't know if I told you about my cousin, Marion? She was overseas with her boyfriend on an extended working holiday when we…when we—'

'You mentioned her in passing, that's all.'

'Oh. Well.' She flicked him a brief glance. 'We used to be very close—she actually came to live with us when her parents died—but she's been overseas for ages. Now they're back, she and Derek, and they're getting married in a fortnight. I'm going to be a bridesmaid.'

'I know.'

Caiti blinked. 'What? I mean, how could you—?'

'I know you're going to be her bridesmaid.'

'How on earth…?' She broke off and stared at him.

His lips twisted. 'I, for my sins, am the best man.'

'You…know…Derek Handy?' Her eyes were huge. 'You *know* my cousin Marion?'

'I have yet to meet Marion but I was at boarding-school with Derek for years.'

Caiti reached for her glass and took a solid sip of brandy. It went down like firewater again but this time it paralysed her vocal cords and she could only open and shut her mouth several times.

Rob Leicester looked amused. 'You don't feel I make good best-man material?'

'No,' she got out at last. 'Well, I have no idea.'

'Or,' he gazed at her narrowly and continued softly but lethally, 'you're wondering how the hell this could have happened to you?'

Caiti breathed raggedly and could only be honest. 'Yes.'

As he watched her, Rob Leicester was presented with a vivid mental picture of the last time he'd had her in his arms. Even in the short space of their relationship he'd discovered that you never knew quite what to expect from her, but one thing had never changed. Her slim, golden body, and all that gorgeous black hair. But it was her stunning lavender eyes, whether they were laughing at him or dreamy

and content, that had tantalised him almost un-
bearably.

'So you didn't come back to Cairns to look me up
at the same time?' he suggested with an undertone
of harshness.

'Rob,' she gestured, 'perhaps, but only after the
wedding.'

'How thoughtful of you,' he drawled.

She closed her eyes then her lashes flew up. 'You
said—for your sins, you were Derek's best man.
What did you mean?'

He shrugged. 'As it happens, I don't particularly
see myself as good best-man material and I would
have found some way of dodging it if it hadn't been
for Derek mentioning who the chief bridesmaid
was—you.'

If only Marion had told me, she thought anguish-
edly. If only I'd thought to ask who the best man
was! But how would that have helped? I could never
have refused to be Marion's bridesmaid...

'As a matter of interest, where have you been over
the last eighteen months, Caiti?' he queried. 'I spent
a small fortune trying to find you, even going so far
as to make enquiries in New Caledonia.'

Caiti flinched. Her French mother came from New
Caledonia and, not long before she'd met Rob, her
parents had separated unexpectedly, her mother returning to her home country. She'd been deeply disturbed by their separation; she adored both her parents. It had often occurred to her that because of it,

she'd been much more vulnerable to being swept off her feet by Rob…

'Uh—my mother reverted to her maiden name,' she said, and avoided the rest of the question. 'How is your brother, Steve?'

'He's fine now but it was a long convalescence.'

'So…so you're back at Camp Ondine?'

He nodded. 'I've just flown in from Cooktown.'

'Rob—'

'Caiti,' he interrupted, 'let's not beat about the bush or indulge in any further mindless pleasantries.' The look he tossed her was laced with pitiless irony. 'You married me then ran away two days later. Shouldn't we be discussing that?'

She put a hand to her mouth. 'You know why.'

'I—' But he broke off as a call came over the loudspeaker system for Miss Caitlin Galloway to proceed to the information desk.

'That must be a message from Marion,' Caiti said. 'She must have been held up.'

He got up. 'I'll go.'

Two minutes later he was back and he handed her a slip of paper. On it was printed the news that Marion had been involved in a minor traffic accident—she was not hurt, but couldn't leave the scene until the police arrived; and would Caiti please take a taxi from the airport to Marion's home…the key was in the same place.

'Look,' she let the paper flutter to the table, 'Mar-

ion has no idea, I haven't seen her in two years...'
She broke off abruptly, then, 'Does Derek know?'

'No,' he said slowly. 'I thought I'd await your wisdom on the subject.'

Her throat worked. 'I can't just spring it on Marion,' she said urgently. 'She'll be horrified.'

'Possibly,' he agreed sardonically.

'You *should* have dodged it,' she accused.

He linked his long, strong fingers. 'That's a matter of opinion.'

'No,' Caiti denied, 'it's not! Anyone could see that it has to cast a shadow over their wedding. Not only that but you're not related to Derek as I am to Marion and you just said you don't see yourself as—'

'By the same token,' he broke in impatiently, 'anyone could see there is unfinished business between us, Caiti, so—'

'There *needn't* be,' she said intensely. 'You could have instituted divorce proceedings through my solicitor, as I wrote and told you just after I left.'

'Your solicitor,' he repeated drily. 'Did you honestly think I would be happy only to communicate with you through your solicitor?'

She swallowed. 'Be that as it may, I don't know what to think now.' She put her hands delicately to her temples.

Rob Leicester watched her closely again. If the truth were known, her Gallic gestures, passed on by her French mother no doubt, had always fascinated him. She used her hands a lot. And he'd always been able to tell when she was disturbed, not only from her hands but also by the way a pulse disturbed the deliciously smooth skin at the base of her slender throat. It was beating rapidly now…

'The sooner you break the news to Marion the better.'

'That's easy for you to say,' she objected. 'She'll probably be hurt that I didn't write to her about it. It was something I just couldn't put in a letter—she may even have decided to come haring home!'

'But you intended to confide in her at this reunion, I imagine?' He studied her critically. 'Or have you decided simply to block it all out of your mind?'

'Of course not!'

Their gazes clashed and his was sardonic as he murmured, 'One could be forgiven for wondering about that.'

She swallowed. 'I—'

'Then the sooner also,' he overrode her, 'you acknowledge that things aren't finished between us, Caiti Leicester,' he said deliberately, 'the better.'

'Things?' she echoed huskily.

He sat back, his hazel gaze terribly mocking. 'Would you have got such a shock to see me again if I meant nothing to you now?'

She bit her lip. 'How long are you in Cairns for?'

'A few days, I'm here on business as well. I believe that in a couple of days' time we're having a get-together; the bridal couple, bridesmaids, best man, Derek's mother, sister and her boyfriend.'

Caiti closed her eyes then her lashes flew up as he laughed softly.

'If you could see your horrified expression,' he said.

'R-Rob,' her voice shook, 'would you have just sprung yourself on me at this get-together if we hadn't bumped into each other today?' she queried.

He considered. 'If necessary, although I doubt you would have gone on in ignorance for that long. I'm actually taking things one day at a time. There was no way of knowing *when* the chief bridesmaid would discover who the best man was.'

'That's diabolical!'

His eyes narrowed and he watched her intently. 'Is it, Caiti? Any more diabolical, would you say, than the way you left Camp Ondine two days after we got married?'

Her lips parted.

He stood up. 'Think about it. In the meantime I'll give you a lift to Marion's.'

Caiti hesitated then stood up too. 'Thank you.'

The drive from the airport to Marion's house was mercifully short. All the same, it was ten tense minutes until he nosed the powerful Range Rover into her cousin's driveway.

He'd said nothing on the way. She'd stared out of the window and observed that little had changed since she'd last been in Cairns. Still the same lush, tropical foliage and flowers, and still the same bird calls that were so evocative of the region.

Then he pulled up and turned to her. 'You wouldn't be so silly as to do another bunk, would you, Caiti?'

She took an angry breath as their gazes clashed. 'There was no silliness involved the first time,' she said tautly.

'But you agree it was a bunk?' he countered with lazy insolence.

'I agree that I was misled,' she said precisely, 'and I found it impossible to carry on in the circumstances. However, no, I won't be doing a bunk, Rob, until we've sorted things out because we obviously can't go on like this.' She opened her door and slipped out of the car. 'Don't worry, I can manage my bag.'

But he got out and retrieved it for her. 'Until the party, then, but I'll give you this should you need to get in touch in the meantime.' He fished a business card out of his pocket and handed it to her.

She didn't even glance at it. 'I won't.'

'You're very proud, Caiti,' he said softly. 'Takes me right back to when we first met—remember?' He waited for a moment as her eyes changed beneath a flood of memories, then he swung himself back into the vehicle, and drove off.

Caiti had just let herself into the house when Marion arrived home with a large dent in her car's front fender.

The cousins fell into each other's arms.

Marion Galloway was short and generously curved with curly brown hair and she had a warm, open nature. At twenty-five, she was two years older than Caiti and an audiologist by profession. Despite losing her parents as a teenager, she had her life well organised and her long relationship with Derek Handy had always run smoothly.

'I've missed you so much!' she said to Caiti as they hugged exuberantly.

'Me too,' Caiti responded. 'How was it? Did you have a marvellous time? I want to hear all about it!' she warned.

'Let's have a cup of tea. Phew!' Marion wiped her brow. 'What an afternoon!'

A few minutes later they were sitting over a cup of tea on the pleasant, creeper-shaded veranda, and Marion was reminiscing about her trip.

'But it's so wonderful to be home,' she said at last. 'It's been six weeks but it's *still* wonderful. I'm only sorry we couldn't have got together earlier.'

'Better this way,' Caiti said. 'I've got a whole month off.'

'Tell me about it! Sounds great, working for the French Embassy in Canberra. Lucky you to have had a French mother.' But Marion sobered rapidly. 'Is there any hope of a reconciliation between your parents?'

Caiti and Marion's father's were brothers.

Caiti heaved a sigh. 'No. I can't quite believe it happened, you know. She's got this new man in her life I don't like at all. Dad is roaming around South America—he's in Patagonia at the moment—and I'm sure he's bereft. They were married for twenty-five *years* when they split up.'

Marion shook her head in dismay. They discussed Caiti's job as an interpreter for a while, and the pleasures of living in the nation's capital.

'It's a long way from Cairns,' Marion said humorously, 'but what made you give up teaching?'

Caiti hesitated because this was heading into difficult territory. How to tell Marion that in very short order her parents had split up while Marion was overseas, and teaching French to mostly bored high-school students had been no balm to her troubled, suddenly lonely soul?

How then to explain that she'd tossed in teaching and taken up tour-guiding, which had virtually led her into Rob Leicester's arms?

'Uh—got bored with it, I guess,' she said ruefully.

'To be honest,' Marion said slowly, 'I never thought you were cut out for teaching languages. You're too artistic.'

Caiti relaxed slightly. 'Well, I've been able to indulge that side of me, if it is there, over the past year in Canberra. I've done a course in French literature at the National University as well as a music-appreciation course. But listen, I want to know all about the wedding plans!'

Marion blew out her cheeks. 'It's been a bit of a rush, to be honest.'

'I—I wondered about that. Two months isn't a lot of time to organise a wedding.'

'Tell me about it!' Marion looked heavenwards. 'But I just knew, as Derek and I were coming home, that now was the time to do it.'

Caiti studied her cousin and frowned inwardly as she wondered why Marion's words had raised a curious little echo in her mind—*now or never?*

And it struck her that Marion and Derek Handy had been together for at least four years, so could Marion be getting a little desperate to tie the knot…?

But Marion continued blithely, 'I think I have it all under control, though. Mind you, it's been a battle. Derek's mother has very decided ideas and since I have no mother of my own she seems to have set herself up as my mother by proxy. There have been a couple of tense times.'

Caiti blinked. 'Such as?'

'She's pink-fixated for one thing. She wanted pink smoke, pink doves, pink bridesmaid's dresses and choirboy angels with pink wings.'

Caiti started to laugh helplessly. 'I don't believe it!'

'Wait until you meet her,' Marion advised. 'However, you and Eloise—she's Derek's sister and the other bridesmaid—will be walking down the aisle in midnight-blue rather than the particularly foul baby-pink she had in mind—all gratitude duly accepted!'

'Thank you so much, Marion! Baby-pink makes me look as if I have jaundice.'

Marion grinned. 'As for the rest of it, it's all fallen into place rather nicely, and Derek is particularly thrilled because the person he most wanted for his best man is available.'

Caiti froze.

It went unnoticed as Marion poured more tea. She added, as she spooned sugar into her cup, 'It was so lucky really, considering what short notice it was and the fact that Rob Leicester moves about quite a lot. Have you heard of Leicester Camps, Caiti?'

'Yes…' Caiti said slowly, and it came out as if she were searching her mind for an elusive name when, in fact, she was searching for a way to break the news to Marion that she had actually married the founder of Leicester Camps then run away from him.

'They've developed a few eco-resorts in remote spots that have really taken off,' Marion supplied. 'Well, Rob has. The family owns a grazing empire on Cape York but Rob—he's the younger son—decided to diversify. The first one he opened was Camp Ondine, north of the Daintree. Apparently it's a magical rainforest and reef experience. Another biscuit?' She offered the plate to Caiti.

Caiti shook her head numbly.

'Anyway, Derek and Rob were at boarding-school together and their friendship carried on from there. I'm not quite sure why but Derek's always admired

Rob Leicester tremendously and to find that he was back at Camp Ondine, and available, was perfect.'

Marion paused and a faint frown knitted her brow. 'In fact, I sometimes think,' she reflected, 'it's the one wedding detail that has Derek's unqualified approval.'

'What do you mean?' Caiti queried with a frown of her own.

Marion shook her head and laughed. 'Nothing. Well, it hasn't been an easy time for poor Derek with his mother and I at loggerheads occasionally. He is her only son and she lost her husband not that long ago. I don't know—I just get the feeling that he's really relying on Rob to get him through it all. I haven't met him myself so I hope he's right. Incidentally, we're having a get-together in a couple of days so we'll all meet the famous Rob Leicester then!'

'Marion—'

But Marion beat her to the draw. 'Honey, you look a bit tired,' she said with concern. 'You've been flying all day and here I am rattling on about Derek's best man! Why don't you have a nice long soak in the tub while I get dinner ready?'

CHAPTER TWO

CAITI ran the bath and sat down to watch the water flowing with utter confusion in her mind.

To parody the words of Rob Leicester, she thought bitterly, how could this have happened to her?

But there were other thoughts. Was she being ultra-sensitive or did she detect that all was not quite as it should be between Marion and Derek?

One thing *was* becoming obvious—Derek would not take kindly to finding a substitute best man. But was Derek actually having second thoughts? Was Marion rushing him into a wedding against his better judgement?

She reached over to turn the taps off then sat back on the bathroom stool as it hit her that all of that paled into insignificance beside her own dilemma— the dilemma of finding that she was as vulnerable to Rob as she'd ever been.

And she had been vulnerable, she reminded herself. Her parents' separation just before she'd met Rob had confused and unsettled her. That she should feel troubled and confused had come as no surprise but at only twenty-one then, the loneliness she'd suffered when her parents had gone their separate ways had come as quite a shock.

To counter it, she'd given up her teaching job after a while and applied for something more challenging. She'd applied for a job as a tour guide and interpreter with a company that specialised in bringing French tourists on conducted trips to Cairns and the tropical delights of Queensland.

She'd got the job despite no previous experience and that was how she'd come to meet Rob.

One segment of the package tour on offer had been a two-night stay at a luxury rainforest camp run by Leicester Camps, a company with a growing reputation for developing eco-camps in remote and beautiful spots.

Camp Ondine had been under Rob's management at the time. North of Cairns on the mouth of a river, it offered not only an unparalleled rainforest experience but also fishing and island-hopping trips offshore to the adjacent Great Barrier Reef. Its maximum capacity was thirty, so it was intimate, and the emphasis was on service and a wonderful cuisine.

Caiti had been most impressed. Then she'd met the man in charge and it had been a bit like receiving a high-voltage charge of electricity.

At thirty then, Rob Leicester was nine years her senior. Not only that, but he'd also first viewed her as a disaster—and told her so.

Her mind took wings as she sat beside Marion's bath, right back to that first encounter…

*   *   *

Caiti regarded the man who had just accused her of being a walking disaster.

He was tall and rugged with thick, dark, slightly shaggy hair and blue shadows on his jaw. He wore jeans and a blue sweatshirt as if, despite owning and running Camp Ondine, he bucked in with his staff and was more a behind-the-scenes operator than a front man.

On the other hand, the jeans and sweatshirt moulded to broad shoulders and a rock-hard body heightened a dynamically masculine presence. The unexpected impact this had on Caiti made her draw an excited little breath, annoyingly.

Above all, he had light hazel eyes that were boring right through her in a singularly insolent and unimpressed manner.

Big, tough, mean and nasty—it shot through her mind.

She was nothing if not resilient, however. 'And you may go to *hell*, Mr Leicester,' she told him with all the hauteur she could muster.

A spark of interest lit Rob Leicester's hazel eyes. 'I see. A rebel without a cause as well.'

'This is my first week on the job,' she replied. 'All I require is a little time to hone my skills.'

'What you require is a qualified tour guide as an assistant, someone to co-ordinate your clients' baggage, their dietary requirements and all the nuts and bolts of the job. So you can just be,' he subjected her person and her long dark hair to a thorough inspection, 'decorative and dazzle us with your French,' he drawled.

'I don't like you,' Caiti stated through her teeth.

A flicker of a grin revealed white teeth in Rob Leicester's tanned face. 'You don't have to and I don't have to like you, Ms Galloway. The fact remains we prepared twelve non-vegetarian dinners last night for twelve subjects of *vive la France!* who are *all* vegetarians because *you* ticked the wrong box.'

Caiti coloured.

'Can you imagine, when the error was discovered, the kind of chaos it caused in the kitchen?'

'I'm sorry,' she said stiffly. 'I was in a rush. May I say that your kitchen coped brilliantly? I've received nothing but compliments from the guests this morning.'

Rob Leicester folded his arms and regarded her impassively for a moment. Then his lips twisted. 'Amazing what a pair of lavender eyes, hair like rough black silk and a very jaunty derrière can do.'

She opened her mouth on a cutting retort then decided to disengage with dignity—she walked away without a backward glance.

On her next encounter with Camp Ondine, she went out of her way to have everything under control but their four-wheel-drive bus broke down in the middle of the Daintree Forest in a tropical downpour. By the time she and the driver were able to organise a replacement vehicle, it was ten tired and very wet tourists she brought to Camp Ondine, four hours later than expected and two hours after the dining room was expecting them for dinner.

Rob Leicester was on hand to greet the party this time and the look he cast her spoke volumes. It was not until her tour was fed and bedded down for the night that Caiti was able to defend herself.

She was making her way wearily across the lounge to her cabin when she bumped into Rob.

'You cannot blame me for a broken differential,' she said, going immediately on the attack.

He shrugged. 'There's a theory that trouble attracts trouble.' Khaki trousers and shirt had replaced the old jeans and sweatshirt tonight.

Caiti opened her mouth to refute his theories but he forestalled her by suggesting they have a drink.

She closed her mouth and said instead, 'Why would I want a drink?'

'Because you're tired, you've had a tough day?' he hazarded.

'Let me rephrase.' She regarded him coolly. 'Why would I want to have a drink with *you*? We don't like each other, remember?'

'That could change. And I never said I didn't like you.'

Caiti blinked and cast her mind back with an effort.

At the same time Rob reached behind a small bar and produced a chilled bottle of wine and a beer.

'What I said,' he opened the wine competently, 'was that we didn't *have* to like each other. Not quite the same thing.'

He poured the wine, popped the beer can and handed her the glass—he literally put it into her hand and closed her fingers around the stem at the same time as he invited her to sit down.

Caiti looked around. The lounge had a thatched roof held up by gnarled tree trunks. The floor was slate, dotted with thick, colourful rugs and there were comfortable settees with softly lit lamps on their end tables. Beyond the glass walls that looked out over the forest, rain dripped ceaselessly off the thatch but that only served to highlight how pleasant, comfortable and *safe* this safari lounge felt.

She sat down with a sigh. 'How do you keep them out?'

He sprawled out opposite her. 'Keep what out?'

'The frogs.' She shuddered. They were everywhere!

'Ah. While you were broken down in the Daintree?'

'Yes.' She sipped her wine. 'It's just as well none of my tour speak much English.'

He grinned. 'You were moved to express yourself colourfully?'

'I was moved to use several words I have never used in my life in public,' she said.

'Some words are—universal.'

She glanced at him through her lashes. 'I hope

not,' she said as his gaze drifted down her figure, now cleanly and drily dressed in slim aubergine trousers with a cream silk fitted blouse.

As it did so, it crossed Rob Leicester's mind that although she was not technically beautiful, she was unusual and compelling. Her face was narrow and oval, her skin golden and her heavy hair, swept up into an elegant knot, was gorgeous, the perfect frame for her face and slender neck. Not only that, but her eyes were also stunning and her presentation was essentially chic.

'How did you get this job?' he enquired then, just as Caiti was starting to feel uneasy beneath his minute scrutiny.

'Because I speak French.'

'That all?' He lifted an eyebrow.

'I also spent three months in France once. And I'm not an idiot,' she replied evenly.

He didn't comment on that. 'What's the French connection?'

'My mother is French, born in New Caledonia. But I was born in Port Douglas.' Port Douglas was not that far from Camp Ondine. 'Something else that made me suitable for this job,' she added with a toss of her head. 'I'm a local.'

'So put that in your pipe and smoke it, Rob Leicester,' he murmured.

Caiti tossed him a deadly little glance although she said smoothly enough, 'What I would really like you to put in your pipe and smoke is this. Circumstance may have made me appear a trifle...silly and less than capable, Mr Leicester. You can go on believing that if you like but it's far from the truth. Good night.'

She drained her glass and stood up.

He followed suit, crumpling his beer can around the middle in one strong hand. 'Good night, Miss Galloway. By the way, we don't always manage to keep the local wildlife out.'

Her eyes widened.

'Would you like me to check your cabin before you retire?'

For a second she was terribly tempted. Then it occurred to her that, mysteriously, there was something more flowing between them. He was studying her assessingly again but this time he was concentrating on her figure.

And beneath that penetrating hazel gaze, her stomach lurched as the full masculine impact of the man hit her. It was a curiously devastating impact. It was as if he was paring things down between them to the fundamentals between a man and a woman. As if they were flesh on flesh, breathing each other's essence, tantalising one another, withholding, granting, testing, fulfilling...

And so powerful was it, she glanced involuntarily down at his hands because she could almost feel them on her breasts, burning through the thin silk of her blouse.

But his expression changed and she was beset by

another impression of Rob Leicester. Rugged, powerful, yes, but perhaps more complex than she'd given him credit for? The lines and angles of his face were interesting, and his eyes, as he looked down into hers, were definitely posing a worldly little question as he suddenly smiled a secret half-smile that was seriously sexy.

Her heart started to hammer, her pulses began to pound and such was her disarray, nothing in the world would have had the power at that moment to distract her from feeling undeniably stirred up by Rob Leicester.

Nor could she doubt that his presence in her cabin wouldn't lead on to...

No, stop right there, Caiti Galloway! she commanded herself and made a desperate bid to take hold.

'Uh, I think I'll take my chances,' she said with an effort. 'Seems safer than...' She closed her eyes and bit her lip.

'Safer than...?'

What you have in mind for me, Rob Leicester, she longed to say, but as her lashes flew up she saw so much amused comprehension in his eyes she could have killed herself.

She tried to look nonchalant and added, as this line of reasoning, although plucked from thin air, nevertheless sounded quite sensible to her ears, 'I'll... manage.' She tilted her chin.

'So, if I hear any maidenly shrieks or unmaidenly

language coming from your cabin, I should just ignore it?' he questioned gravely.

'*Yes.*' This time her lavender gaze was dangerous.

'So be it,' he murmured. 'I am right next door, however, should your…new-found bravery desert you. Good night, Miss Galloway.' He turned away and left the lounge.

Which was fortunate as Caiti found herself rooted to the spot. The thought of Rob Leicester sleeping right next door to her, if he'd meant what she'd thought he meant, was infinitely disturbing. The cabin she'd been allotted this time was a duplex. Two *en suite* rooms with one dividing wall and a shared veranda…

She came alive a moment later, shook her head and posed a question to herself—was she going crazy? She'd only met the man *twice* and both times in difficult if not to say demoralising circumstances!

The militant mood of disbelief this conversation had fostered in her boded ill for any future meetings with Mr Leicester. She undressed, got into bed and arranged the mosquito net then composed herself for sleep.

There was no sound from the other cabin, no light, so she guessed her tormentor had not yet gone to bed, but there were a million frogs croaking away outside to reactivate her memories of being broken down in the Daintree.

I'll never sleep, she thought despairingly, then stiffened as she heard footsteps outside and the lightest rap on her door at the same time as Rob Leicester said softly, 'You all right there, Miss Galloway?'

Strangely, a little ripple of relief ran through her.

'I'm fine, Mr Leicester. Quite fine, thank you so much!' she replied.

'Sleep well, then,' he said and she heard his door open and close.

She did just that.

Any slight spirit of unity with Rob Leicester was gone the next morning.

He took the fast launch trip to the Hope Isles, which six of her party, all men, elected to go on. Caiti's services were needed on the launch, as an interpreter. Rob was most professional both when they stopped to fish and when they went ashore—for the most part. He concentrated on the guests, and left Caiti nearly single-handedly to serve up the picnic lunch.

It was a glorious day. The rain had gone, the sea was calm, a pale, shimmering blue, they weren't far off-shore so the dark green mountainous scenery of the mainland was magnificent, and the fish were biting.

Despite the language constraints, the camaraderie of seven men catching fish was soon evident. So was their enthusiasm. It crossed her mind to think once that they hadn't really needed her, there was obviously a universal language amongst fishermen. It also crossed her mind to think that she was being unfairly exposed to Rob Leicester.

He drove the launch with consummate skill. He seemed to know all there was to know about the art of catching fish, where to find them and how to clean them. Once, she caught a quizzical little sideways glance from him as he gutted a red emperor with the minimum of fuss.

But her squeamishness did not extend to fish, dead or alive. Her parents had run a restaurant in Port Douglas for years and she'd been well-schooled by her mother and her father in all aspects of fish cookery, from catching and cleaning them through to buying them in the market and cooking them.

Got you there, she said to him in her mind as she picked up a headless fish, borrowed a knife and filleted it neatly before consigning the fillets to the ice chest.

This earned her a round of applause from her party but no particular approbation from Rob Leicester.

When they landed on the lovely islet called Hope, a circle of white sand with a crown of thick bush and trees, he explained briefly where and how to set up the picnic lunch, and took the rest of the party on a tour of the island, the coral and for a swim.

Blow you, Mr Leicester, she said to him in her mind again as she stripped to her amethyst bikini and had a quick swim in the crystal-clear water herself.

She dried herself and pulled on her white shorts but didn't cover up her bikini top. She loosened her hair to allow it to dry, began to set out lunch and was waiting demurely beside it when the party returned. They all tucked in with gusto, full of enthusiasm for the Hope Isles and full of questions for her that they'd been unable to put to Rob.

Another feather in my cap, Mr Leicester—she beamed the thought at him while maintaining her severely demure demeanour—and this time got a response.

He squinted at her through his damp dark hair. 'You look like the cat that's got the cream, Miss Galloway,' he observed, as she poured piping hot coffee from a flask.

'Cream? Cat?' one of her party enquired. 'What means ziss, Mlle Caiti?'

She smiled delightfully at the middle-aged man. 'He thinks I'm,' she paused, 'very competent,' she said instead of trying to explain that Rob Leicester thought she was downright smug.

'Bravo!' And a stream of French followed indicating that they all thought so too.

'*Merci!*' Caiti turned back to Rob and said rapidly, 'They don't think I'm smug at all.'

'So I gathered.' He crossed his arms and looked at her moodily. 'What exactly did you tell them?'

She glanced around but everyone had wandered off. She explained and added, 'I didn't try to lower you in the popularity stakes.' Her smile, this time, was virtuous.

'Thank you, but it doesn't bother you to go around misrepresenting things?'

Caiti grimaced. 'You could have had a riot on your hands otherwise,' she said simply.

'And it has been known for pride to come before a fall,' he retorted swiftly.

'Is it only me or are you always so full of these theories?' she queried, still smiling delightfully. 'If it's only me, I wonder what I have to do to persuade you otherwise.'

'One swallow doesn't make a summer. I'll reserve judgement.' He got up and began to pack up the picnic.

She watched him for a moment. Another sweatshirt was moulded over his hard muscles above shorts that exposed long, powerful legs. Once again her stomach lurched…

To counter it, she said, 'You can also go to hell again, Mr Leicester!' And she waltzed down to the water's edge.

But inside she was seething, and confused, she realised. The trials and tribulations of yesterday had not been her fault; they could have happened to anyone. So, the only thing he had to hold against her was one mistake from the previous tour. Did that warrant being so…disliked as she felt she was today? And what about last night?

She stopped rather suddenly and thought—was this all to do with her refusing to acknowledge the *frisson* that had undoubtedly existed between them?

Well, well, she mused, in that case it's about time more women said no to you, Rob Leicester!

They didn't stop to fish on the way back to the camp and got there at about four-thirty, which left her with an hour or so of free time before the fish barbecue, using the day's catch.

She let herself into her cabin thankfully as she realised how tired she was. A lot of sun and sea air on top of a stressful day yesterday, she reasoned, and thought, with a wry smile, that you needed the constitution of an ox to be a tour guide.

She showered, donned a colourful cotton wrap, made herself a cup of tea then could no longer resist the invitations her crisp white bed was sending out. Just forty winks, she promised herself as she lay down. Twenty minutes at the most and she'd be up and about, all bright-eyed and bushy-tailed.

An hour and a half later she sat up with a hand to her throat, no idea where she was, then aware that someone was knocking on the door. It was dark, and suddenly it all came back to her...

She flew off the bed and ran to the door, praying it wouldn't be Rob Leicester come to find out what had happened to her, but of course it was. This time he was sleek and combed and in front-man mode in clean jeans and shirt.

'Oh, no! I'm late, aren't I? I just fell into this... this...deep sleep,' she gabbled as she clutched her wrap with one hand and gathered her long loose hair with the other. 'Damn! I suppose this makes you *happy*?'

He raised his eyebrows. 'Why should it do that?'

'One of your theories has come home to roost, that's why. One swallow doesn't make a summer,' she mimicked with some bitterness.

'On the contrary, I would have been quite happy to let you sleep on, Miss Galloway,' he drawled. 'Your party had other ideas. They want you there at the barbecue and celebrating their last night at Camp Ondine. I don't know if they're prepared to riot about it but I thought I shouldn't take the chance.'

Caiti stared up into his eyes. Then she looked down at herself. 'I feel terrible!'

'This is only a small dereliction of duty so far, I wouldn't feel too badly,' he advised.

'No.' She swallowed. 'I mean I feel leaden and lumpen and as bad as you only *can* after a deep, wrong-time-of-the-day sleep.'

'I see. I wouldn't have thought it was possible for you to feel lumpen,' his gaze flickered up and down her slender lines beneath her wrap, 'but I think I could remedy all the rest. Wait here.' He turned away.

Wait here, she repeated beneath her breath. *Yes, sir, no, sir, three bags full, sir!* How autocratic could you get?

She had to eat her thoughts not much later when he returned with a tall, frosted glass and put it into her hand.

'What's this?' she asked suspiciously.

'Don't ask. It's a fantastic pick-me-up. On top of a shower and,' his lips twisted, 'a more formal state of dress, you should be fine. You have half an hour; I'll hold the fort in the meantime.' This time he closed the door before departing.

Caiti stared at the door then at the drink in her hand, and took a sip. It was divine whatever it was and definitely had mango and other juices poured over crushed ice with some slivers of lime in it.

She took a bigger sip and could have sworn it was her imagination, but suddenly she no longer felt like something the cat had dragged in.

In fact, she glided into the bathroom, had another quick shower, donned her undies then sat down at the dressing table with approaching enthusiasm. Several minutes and a few more sips later, her light make-up was perfect and even her hair was behaving itself. She drew it back in two wings, secured with a pretty silver and enamelled butterfly on a clip, and allowed the rest of it to cascade down her back loose.

Clothes, she thought then, and decided to go with her aubergine trousers, low silver sandals and a silver knit tank top. Simple but chic, she decided as she posed in front of the mirror and twirled so her hair belled out. Then she paused suddenly and regarded the half-empty glass on the dressing table.

Could it be as innocuous a brew as he'd intimated? Was it possible to go from feeling quite dreadful to feeling on top of the world in the space of about twenty minutes without being a little drunk? Which led on to her wondering just what kind of man Rob Leicester was.

She blinked several times and came to one decision. She would not be having any more of his pick-me-up.

The fish was just ready to be served when she arrived at the barbecue beside the pool, and she received a rousing welcome.

She offered her apologies but they were brushed aside and, somehow or other, she ended up as the guest of honour. She couldn't help wondering what effect this status was having on Rob Leicester, who had actually done the cooking.

But there were staff members to do the serving, several colourfully clad waitresses with flowers in their hair, and it was a feast every bit worthy of Camp Ondine's reputation.

Not only that but some fine wines were also flowing and earning the respect of her tour party. Caiti didn't indulge herself but beneath a marvellous array of stars, with flaming braziers lighting the barbecue area, she felt happy and fulfilled to see the guests really enjoying themselves.

It must have something to do with me, she assured herself, and sent a swift little prayer heavenwards that the rest of this tour would be as successful.

Then, when the guests began to sing the 'Marseillaise', she joined in with gusto, and perfect pitch, but insisted that since they were in Australia they should at least be able to sing 'Waltzing Matilda'.

There followed an hilarious half-hour while she tried to translate but finally, although with some very strange pronunciation, she got a not bad rendition of a couple of verses, helped along by Rob and the staff who joined in.

Finally she glanced at her watch and decided it was timely to mention that they had an early start in the morning. Everyone groaned but gradually they took themselves off to bed.

'A successful evening, Miss Galloway.'

Caiti looked up from the paperwork she was checking at the reception desk; she was determined to leave all the correct vouchers so there could be no confusion in the morning. 'Thanks to you and your wonderful food, Mr Leicester,' she replied formally. 'It's also a marvellous spot.'

'Oh, I don't know about that.' He folded his arms and leant back against a wall.

'What's that supposed to mean?' A tinge of sharpness overlaid some of her formality.

'I've revised an opinion or two.'

She shrugged. 'I'm sure it's good for one to shake up one's opinions now and then. Which ones?'

He took his time. In other words he looked her over thoroughly as he had an uncanny habit of doing before he said, 'I think you could charm the birds out of the trees.'

Their unsmiling gazes locked until Caiti said slowly, 'Why do I get the feeling that's not exactly a compliment?'

'I have no idea.'

'Then I'll tell you,' she returned swiftly. 'I'm quite sure "charm" is not a commodity you value.'

'What gave you that idea?'

'Oh, come on!' She closed her eyes briefly. 'Let's not beat about the bush. You don't like me, you're quite sure I'm trading on "charm" to get this job done, and by the way—what did you put in that drink you brought me?'

His eyes narrowed. 'Nothing alcoholic bar a dash of Grenadine. Are you saying I tried to get you drunk?'

She paused and bit her lip. 'It…certainly revived me.'

'So I noticed.' His eyes glinted with a tinge of mockery. 'I can assure you there was nothing more to it.'

'Well,' she hesitated, feeling as if she'd had the wind taken out of her sails, 'well, even if you didn't try to get me drunk, I'm sick and tired of your continuous disapproval.'

'It's not all disapproval, Miss Galloway.' He straightened and stepped forward.

Caiti's eyes widened and she rather hastily moved a few steps so the desk was between them at the same time as she shook a finger at him. 'Now, now, Mr Leicester, none of that!'

Rob Leicester stopped dead, and started to laugh softly.

Completely disconcerted, Caiti blinked several times. 'It's not funny!'

'No, but you are. Is that how you fight them off?'

'Off? Who?'

'All the men on your tours who fancy you rotten,' he suggested.

'It might interest you to know that that problem has never reared its ugly head,' she replied tartly.

'Only a matter of time.'

Caiti felt herself beginning to lose her temper completely. 'Will you just go away, Mr Leicester, and stop tormenting me?'

'Sure,' he said easily. 'But just so as there is no misunderstanding, Miss Galloway, I may not approve of you entirely but I do,' he leant over the desk and took her chin lightly in his fingers, 'fancy you.'

Their eyes locked, and the gold-flecked depths of his were filled with irony. Then he released her and strolled away.

'And it may interest you to know, Mr Leicester,' she said coldly and clearly, and waited until he stopped and turned back to her, 'that if I were a man, I'd *knock* you to the floor!'

She swept her paperwork into her briefcase and strode away with her hair flying and serious anger in her heart.

He caught her before she was able to leave the

reception area and there followed an undignified little struggle.

'Just,' he caught her wrists finally, 'just *listen*! I'm sorry. That wasn't a very nice thing to say.'

Caiti was panting from her exertions and this caught her off guard. She stopped struggling and did a double take.

He observed her surprise with a wry glint in his eyes and added, 'I apologise unreservedly. But some women do trade on their looks and their figures.'

'There's not a great deal to trade on, I wouldn't have thought!'

'Then you thought wrong, Miss Galloway,' he said gravely. 'You may not be classically beautiful but you have a wonderful, slender litheness in the way you move, you're the essence of chic, your hands, hair and eyes are stunningly beautiful and you have an irresistible personality.'

'So why…?'

'I've just worked out that it's genuine.'

'Because I wanted to knock you down?'

He nodded ruefully. 'With very real longing in your voice.'

Caiti took an unexpected breath, and he released her wrists.

She rubbed them involuntarily.

'Sorry about that too,' he said barely audibly.

'Apologies accepted,' she replied rather breath-lessly, 'although—'

'You're right,' he broke in. 'Let's not jump the

gun even if all misunderstandings have been cleared up. When are you due back at Camp Ondine, Miss Galloway?'

'Uh...' she did some rapid mental calculations '...uh...in a fortnight, I think.'

He smiled his secret half-smile at her. 'May we begin to get to know each other better then?'

She hesitated. 'What did you have in mind?'

'Oh, serious seduction.'

Her lips parted. 'I was afraid of that but I don't seduce easily.'

He raised an eyebrow. 'Good for you. That only popped out because you looked—so extremely cautious. What I really had in mind was snatching a quiet moment to have a drink and a chat. Perhaps we could call it a "ceasefire"?'

Her expression remained cautious.

'Still don't approve?' He looked down at her quizzically.

'I guess I'm still a bit confused,' she told him honestly.

There was a slight pause, then, 'May I ask how old you are, Miss Galloway?'

'Twenty-one.'

A flicker of surprise crossed his eyes.

'You took me for older,' she reproved. 'Not very gallant, Mr Leicester.'

'My apologies, yes, I did, but I deny that it wasn't a compliment. You have a mature aura—was what I meant.'

'You mean when I'm not running late and ticking the wrong boxes?' she countered, unable to hide a smile any longer.

He laughed. 'Perhaps I should say no more other than—I will be here in a fortnight, so, in the meantime, take care, Miss Galloway.'

'Oh, I will,' she assured him. 'By then I should also have the hang of all the nuts and bolts of the job.'

A knock on the bathroom door brought her back to the present.

'You OK, Caiti?' Marion called.

She leapt off the stool and cleared her throat. 'Uh—fine. I won't be long!'

'Take as long as you like—I just thought you might have fallen asleep. But Derek will be here shortly.'

Marion's footsteps moved away and Caiti stripped and stepped into the bath to find that it had gone cold—as cold as she felt beneath the weight of her memories.

CHAPTER THREE

DEREK HANDY greeted Caiti with less than his usual reserve when she finally appeared.

He and Marion were sitting on the veranda over drinks and canapés and he got up to embrace her. 'Long time no see but you haven't changed a bit, Caiti,' he said warmly, and pulled out a chair for her.

'Neither have you, Derek,' she responded with a laugh, then sighed with pleasure as he handed her a gin and tonic. 'I can't tell you how pleasant it is to be back in the tropics sipping a G and T! The one thing I'll never get used to in Canberra is the cold weather.'

But as they chatted amiably for the next half-hour, Caiti found herself focusing on Derek as she remembered the undercurrents she'd sensed in Marion earlier.

Derek Handy had always been something of an enigma to Caiti. She didn't doubt that he was highly intelligent, and she could understand that he and Marion had a lot in common. But he wasn't easy in company and she'd always suspected Derek had a chip on his shoulder, although about what she'd never been able to put her finger on.

Now, perhaps prompted by her two-year absence,

it came to her with sudden clarity that Derek might despair of his thick glasses and already receding hairline, his medium height and uneasy ways in company. Which would also explain, it came to her out of the blue, his admiration for Rob Leicester.

But would it explain any reservations he might have about the wedding? she wondered, and took an unexpected little breath. Perhaps there was a little role reversal going on here that he didn't appreciate? As in, Marion up to very recently being the most compliant of partners but now, to put it crudely, wielding the whip?

I'm probably imagining it all, Caiti thought, and shook her head. I am, to put it mildly, a nervous wreck on my own account—and right on cue, as they were tucking into their pasta dinner, Derek brought up the subject of his best man.

'We're having a little party in a couple of days,' he informed Caiti. 'So you can meet my mum, my sister and Rob. Has Marion told you about him?'

'Of course I have, darling. He is your knight in shining armour, after all,' Marion said.

Derek went still then turned to his bride-to-be. 'What's that supposed to mean?'

Marion widened her eyes at him. 'The best man from heaven?' she suggested. 'I must say I hope he lives up to your high expectations.'

Caiti held her breath as the pleasant evening atmosphere was suddenly laden with tension.

'Marion,' Derek got up, 'you've been making

snide remarks about Rob Leicester ever since I brought his name up. I will not have any more of it,' he said precisely, and he strode down the steps, slammed his car door and reversed out of the drive at speed.

Caiti closed her mouth and turned to her cousin, who had silent tears streaming down her face.

'Honey,' she said gently, 'what's going on?'

'I don't know,' Marion wept. 'He's changed for some reason but I don't know why and it's killing me.'

Caiti got up and put her arms round the other girl. Presently she said to her, 'Have *you* changed—I mean do you still want to marry Derek?'

'Yes!' It came out emphatically despite the tears. 'I've wanted to marry him for years. I know,' she sniffed and lifted her head, 'you've wondered about him sometimes, Caiti. I know there can be times when he's prickly and difficult but when it's only the two of us, we just—click!'

Caiti stroked Marion's hair and considered her options. Tell her cousin that her insistence on this rushed wedding was possibly eroding Derek's masculine ego—but how sure was she, Caiti, of that? Or try to defuse things with some common sense.

She chose the second option because she couldn't doubt the genuine quality of Marion's anguish.

'Here's what I think,' she said slowly as she went back to her chair. 'Lead-ups to weddings are probably always difficult, and because this is a bit rushed it's made it worse. We need to work out a way so you can both relax and enjoy the next couple of weeks.'

'How?' Marion asked tautly.

'Well, you've got me here now for one thing. And,' she smiled across the table, 'there must be so much we can all do together. I'm not,' she waved a hand, 'talking wedding preparations. But we could go up to Palm Cove for lunch, maybe take in the Port Douglas markets, things like that. Really enjoy ourselves in other words and release some of the pressure at the same time.'

'Oh, Caiti,' Marion sighed, 'thank heavens for you! I was beginning to think I should have just marched Derek to the registry office and done the deed.'

Caiti flinched inwardly. Not only because that might have compounded Marion's problems but also if ever there had been a case of marry in haste and repent at leisure, she had done exactly that.

'I guess I'll have to take another stand on Rob Leicester, though. I don't know why,' Marion paused and frowned, 'but without quite realising it I *have* come to resent him and I haven't even met him yet.'

'Could…could you be a little jealous?' Caiti asked hesitantly.

Marion considered then sat up straight and shrugged. 'Perhaps I am.'

Caiti stared at her and felt her heart sink to her boots. How on earth could she introduce her connection with the best man into this minefield without making Marion like him all the less?

'What?' Marion asked.

'Nothing,' Caiti said hastily. 'Look, why don't you go after Derek and sort things out? I'll be fine. Then tomorrow, we can draw up some plans.'

Marion hesitated then she got up and kissed the top of Caiti's head. 'I'll do just that. Thanks. You're a pal in a million.'

'Uh—don't be too hard on him,' Caiti recommended with a quirky little grin. 'Most men like to think they're in command.'

'Most men have egos like eggshells,' Marion quipped back. 'Don't worry, I shall tread gingerly!'

As soon as Marion had driven off, however, Caiti threw pride to the wind and dug into her purse to retrieve the card Rob had given her. She felt she had to tell him what had literally just blown up in her face.

But she got a recorded message to say that he was not available until the next morning. She was about to crumple the card in extreme frustration when his voice overrode the answering-machine.

'Leicester.'

'Oh, Rob!' she said gratefully.

'Caiti?'

'Yes, yes. Look, is there any chance of us talking? Things have got complicated.'

'Have you told Marion?'

'No. That's what I mean about complicated.'

There was a pause, then, 'OK. Where?'

She looked around and realised she felt stifled and restless. 'Somewhere we could walk first?' she suggested.

'I'll pick you up in about half an hour.'

Caiti changed out of her long, summery dress into shorts, and penned a note to Marion saying she'd decided to look up an old friend.

Then she sat on the veranda to wait for Rob, only to find more memories filtering into her mind. Memories of how she'd fallen in love with and married Rob Leicester…

For her next few tours to Camp Ondine after their ceasefire, Rob had been as good as his word. Before going to bed they'd got into the habit of sharing a nightcap on their communal veranda and talking. When they'd worked together, a sense of camaraderie had developed between them and, gradually, the suspicion and confusion with which she'd viewed this undeniably attractive but puzzling, sometimes moody man had waned.

It was also when she'd learnt more about him but at the same time discovered a reticence about his background. She had learnt that the Leicester family had a grazing empire on Cape York Peninsula, that Rob was the younger of two sons and that he'd apparently turned his back on being a cattleman in favour of diversifying the family fortune through tourism ventures.

She'd thought, although he hadn't said it, that there might be a rift in the family because she seemed to detect a slight nuance in any familial references he made and those were admittedly few. She'd even thought about asking him but something had given her the impression she would be warned off. She'd conceded to herself later—too late—that this was a very private man who had resolutely walled off parts of his heart.

At the time, these fleeting impressions had sunk almost as quickly as they'd come to her.

They'd never lacked things to talk about. Her natural bubbliness, her sometimes zany views of life seemed to strike a chord with him. They'd discovered they shared a love of music, Caiti had revealed that all sorts of art fascinated her, and their sense of humour ran along the same lines.

With the benefit of hindsight, though, she'd realised, again too late, that she may have appeared a lot more worldly and exotic than she actually was.

Of course, it had all been so exotic, she'd often mused. What had grown between them had been like some precious, subtle hothouse bloom, nurtured by the exotic surrounds of Camp Ondine. And strengthened more by separation than actual time spent together.

Even so, she had been aware that there were two sides to Rob. He could be a cool, tough businessman with very high standards that occasionally moved the less experienced of his staff to tears. Or there was the freer, younger side to him that made her laugh and love being in his company.

The other thing that encouraged her blossoming relationship with Rob was her lack of family at the time. The aching sadness of her parents' separation had waned with Rob's company and she'd no longer felt so alone in the world.

Then, the slow ripening of their romance had speeded up into something that was almost too hot to handle. To be working beside him decorously was no longer to be played like a piquant game, it was a growing torture. To only be available to each other on an irregular basis was hell.

The night their romance was consummated would always stay with her…

It was nearly midnight before she got the last of her tour party bedded down; it was a particularly lively tour, this one. She stopped as she wandered down the moonlit path to her cabin, to pluck a tiny, starry orchid spray growing on a tree and tuck it behind her ear.

Rob hadn't been in camp when they'd arrived, he'd been in Cooktown trying to get an outboard motor fixed for one of the launches, and she didn't know if he was back yet. But she'd dressed for him in a long, pale blue skirt with a matching strapless top and a lovely, filmy overblouse patterned with flowers.

She swished her skirt as she started walking again, feeling restless because she hadn't seen him for ten days and didn't know if she would see him tonight.

Then she noticed a faint glow coming from the veranda of their duplex cabin and her heart started to beat a little tattoo as her steps quickened.

Rob was waiting for her on the veranda with a candle lit and a bottle of champagne in a silver cooler.

He stood up as she hesitated at the bottom of the steps, and held out his hand. She climbed the steps and put her hand in his.

'How...nice to see you,' she said inadequately.

'And more than nice to see you, Miss Galloway.' He raised her knuckles to his lips and held them there for a long moment, then released her to pour the champagne.

But as she leant against the rail and sipped hers Caiti couldn't control the trembling that had overtaken her, brought on by the things just being in his company did to her, and she spilled some champagne down her blouse.

Rob put his glass down and took her in his arms. 'What?' he said softly.

'I was afraid I mightn't see you this trip,' she confided.

He released her but only to remove her damp overblouse. Then he stroked her bare shoulders and arms. 'It mattered?'

'It mattered,' she whispered. 'These days, every moment I don't see you matters.'

'Same here,' he murmured, then took his hands from her body deliberately. 'To the extent that I have two options at the moment. If I'm to keep my hands off you, I need to go away again. Or...' He left it unsaid but as he stared down into her lavender eyes, his meaning was clear.

She lifted his hand and kissed his palm. 'I think I might die by degrees if you go away, Rob. Please don't.'

He hesitated. 'Are you sure?'

She could only nod but with her heart in her eyes.

He swept her up and carried her into his room.

He also swept away any nerves she legitimately had as he undressed her slowly and celebrated her body with a touch that drove her wild.

As he was kissing her, he hooked his fingers beneath her top and pulled it down to reveal her breasts then held her away.

'Mmm,' he murmured, 'high, ripe and gorgeous, just as I pictured them.'

Her hair had come adrift and was swinging free halfway down her back as she looked up at him. 'You pictured them?'

'Constantly, from the day I first met you, Miss Galloway.'

'Oh.' She looked fleetingly amazed then amused.

His hands moved round to her hips. 'Also these.' He cupped her buttocks. 'But I may have mentioned them.'

'You did. But I wasn't in the mood to appreciate the comment at the time,' she recalled.

'No, you were not.' His fingers found the zip of her skirt, and it floated down her legs, and he made a more intimate exploration of her hips, inadequately protected by a flimsy pair of bikini briefs.

Caiti breathed erratically.

'How about now?' he asked softly.

She looked into his hazel eyes. 'Now?' She brought her hands up and smoothed his shirt front. 'I have to say I think things are a little one-sided at the moment. May I?' she asked with her fingers on a button.

'Be my guest.'

As she unbuttoned his shirt, it came to her that she'd often seen Rob Leicester clad only in shorts, and often been mesmerised, much as she'd tried to hide it, by his broad shoulders, his hard, honed diaphragm and long legs. But as his shirt came off, revealing his muscled chest and the very masculine mat of brown hair on it, the urge to rub her bare breasts against him was uncontrollable and intensely erotic.

It had the same effect on Rob. He growled her name beneath his breath and held her away again so he could tug gently at each burgeoning nipple with his teeth until she wove her fingers through his hair in an unspoken plea to be taken.

It was not a plea he acceded to immediately. He finished undressing them both swiftly and laid her on the bed. What followed, the way he caressed and kissed her body, brought them both an almost unendurable pitch of desire. And on Caiti's part, there was only a momentary hesitation when the final act came, the act of ownership and surrender, before she was swept away with the kind of rapture she'd only ever imagined before.

It was the most complete experience, and she lay in his arms afterwards, and said with a little sigh of pure pleasure, 'That was so amazing. You are so amazing, Mr Leicester. Can I…can I tell you what came to mind just now?'

'Be my guest.'

'Music. It just seemed to pour through me.'

A smile crept into his eyes, and he asked quizzically. 'Can you explain?''

'It was lively and made me feel gorgeous,' she moved luxuriously against him, 'and…I can't find any more words for it.'

'Miss Galloway,' he raised his head and propped it on his elbow so he could see her slim, silky, tumbled length beside him by the candlelight highlighting the glorious swatch of her long dark hair, 'I am without words to describe you.'

'You could tell me I'm no longer a walking disaster,' she suggested gravely.

'I could tell you that,' he agreed, 'but it's not so far from the truth. In that,' he put a hand on her waist as she went still, 'you're exquisite enough to lure many a man onto the rocks. But why didn't you tell me?'

'That I was a virgin?' she said after a little pause.

'Yes.' He took his hand from her waist and stroked her hair.

She thought for a moment. 'I guess you made me feel so wonderful, I didn't need to,' she said slowly then posed a question. 'What difference would it have made?'

'It might have…' He stopped, then gathered her close and pulled the cover up.

He never did tell her what he'd been about to say. And it was only later in the most painful way, that she was to discover that Rob Leicester would never have slept with her if he'd known she was a virgin…

Within days of their sleeping together and before they'd had a chance to discuss the future, two things happened. The company Caiti worked for ceased operations overnight in Australia and she was out of a job. The day before she got word of it, Rob's elder brother, Steve, suffered an accident whilst mustering a bull, an accident that looked as if it would claim his life.

That was when Rob made a suggestion Caiti could only be in complete agreement with.

She'd rung him to tell him her news, only to discover that he'd flown down to Cairns to be at the Base Hospital, to which his brother had been transferred. They met for dinner.

Despite his concern about his brother, her radiant joy at seeing him again was obvious and he held her hard in his arms.

'Caiti,' he said softly into her hair, 'you look like someone who's been given the moon.' He paused and frowned over the top of her head.

'That's how I feel,' she confessed. 'Mind you, it's four days, six hours and thirty-five minutes since the moon fell into my lap so I'm also missing you terribly.'

He held her away and stared into her eyes. That he came, at the same time, to a momentous decision was not revealed to Caiti until the next morning when he took her out for coffee and asked her to marry him.

The coffee shop, not far from the hospital, seemed to tilt before her eyes. 'Are you…are you serious?'

'Extremely serious,' he said. 'But I must warn you there are things in my past that should be explained. For the future, though, I need you, Caiti Galloway.' He paused briefly and his eyes searched hers. 'Would I be right in thinking you need me?'

It didn't even cross her mind at the time that she took this as a euphemism for saying—I love you. And he went on to explain he would have to leave Leicester Camps for the time being and go back to run the family cattle station in Steve's place.

What occupied her mind was a sudden rush of emotion on top of the incredible high she was still feeling after their lovemaking. She looked into her heart and decided that she loved Rob Leicester deeply despite the whirlwind nature of their coming together. And that the logical progression from their physical unity should only lead one way, to the altar.

She came to the conclusion that the fact he saw it the same way made her the happiest girl on the planet. She didn't even think about the walls she'd sensed in him, the intuition she'd occasionally had that he was a very private man who might be hard to get to know completely...

She said yes.

'Caiti, about the things in my past—'

She put her hands over his. 'Rob, what's past is past, I don't need to hear it. It's the future that matters.'

It was only days afterwards, though, that she discovered why he'd asked her to marry him. Her whole world fell apart and she left him.

Over the next few months, she tortured herself with all the little alarm bells she'd missed at the time.

Why hadn't *something* warned her that Rob Leicester would not allow himself to be dashed on the rocks of desire for a woman? Why hadn't the private walls she'd sensed in him alerted her to the depths within him that she couldn't begin to guess about? Why hadn't she stopped to think that *need* and *love* were two different things entirely?

At the time, she put herself out of his reach by going to visit her mother in New Caledonia. It was not a success, though, as she was unable to confide in her. It was also the time—when she realised she was riding an awful treadmill of love, hate, anger, despair, misery and a lack of self-esteem—that she knew she had to start a new life.

Then the job at the French Embassy came up and she'd moved to Canberra. Interesting, busy, cosmopolitan, it had been a lifesaver.

She came back to the present on Marion's veranda, two weeks before her cousin's wedding, and knew that interesting, busy and cosmopolitan it may have been but it had also fooled her into thinking she was over Rob Leicester.

The thought had no sooner entered her mind than he turned his Range Rover into the drive.

CHAPTER FOUR

'SORRY, that took a bit longer than I expected,' he said as he waited for her at the bottom of the steps.

Caiti walked down to him slowly, wishing herself a million miles away rather than in this man's presence with her memories of their lovemaking so close to her. Then she blinked because he was more formally dressed than she'd ever seen him, in a long-sleeved white and grey pinstriped shirt, a tie, pressed charcoal trousers and polished black shoes.

'Have I—taken you away from something important?' she queried.

He shrugged. 'A business dinner I was just about to go to when you rang. It took a bit of extricating myself from it.'

'I'm sorry.'

'It doesn't matter.' He waited while she climbed into the Range Rover then closed the door for her. 'Where's Marion?' he asked as he reversed out of the drive.

'Gone to see Derek. They…had a slight falling out.'

'Over you and me?'

'Not precisely. Rob,' she turned to him impulsively, 'is there any reason we can't pretend we're strangers until after the wedding?'

He flicked her a sardonic little glance. 'Plenty, I would have thought.'

She folded her hands. 'Believe me, it would save an awful lot of drama.'

'It could add a whole lot of drama, Caiti,' he said drily. 'You never know who you could bump into over the next couple of weeks. How would Marion feel about hearing it from other sources?'

She slumped a little in her seat. 'You're right. It's just—well, you're not going to believe what they're fighting about.'

They'd reached the Pier precinct by this time and he nosed the Range Rover into a parking space and raised an eyebrow at her. 'You still want to walk before we talk?'

'Yes. Yes, please,' she said gratefully.

But things had changed, she discovered. Next to the Pier, with its hotel, shopping mall, marina and restaurants overlooking Trinity Inlet, there had been a park.

There was still a park but it had changed so much, she stopped dead in surprise.

'What's this?'

'Cairns' new waterfront look. An improvement, wouldn't you say, on the old, low-tide mud-flat?'

Caiti gazed at the huge white sand and salt-water lagoon with its fountains, distinctive lights, its happy swimmers and lawn surrounds dotted with barbecue huts. 'It sure is!' she said bemusedly.

'Of course, the old mud-flat at low tide is still there beyond the breakwater wall,' he added, 'but they reckon this lagoon has persuaded backpackers to stay another four or five days in Cairns.'

'I can believe it—it's great! But a little public.'

He glanced down at her. She wore a long-sleeved blue shirt and hiking boots with her shorts. 'We can still walk on the other side.'

So they threaded their way past the lagoon and she started to stride out.

He kept up easily but at last, as they came to a bench, she hesitated then plonked herself down on it.

He sat down beside her and waited a few minutes while she caught her breath, then, 'So?'

She looked through the twinkling lights dotted around this more deserted area of the park and marshalled her thoughts. And as well as she was able to, she explained what had happened, adding her own perceptions of the tensions at work beneath the surface of the Galloway-Handy wedding.

'Let me see if I've got this straight,' he said rather bemusedly. 'You think Marion is rushing Derek into this wedding against his better judgement. She's also fighting with his mother, she's *jealous* of me, although she's never met me because she feels I'm exerting some kind of undue influence over him. Should these two be getting married in the first place?' he asked with a streak of dry humour.

'They've been together for four years.'

'I know that. Because they were away for so long, you tend to forget.' He said it thoughtfully but didn't enlarge further.

'The thing is, she's going to like you even *less* when she finds out about us, and Derek is just as liable to call the wedding off if he can't have you as his best man,' Caiti said.

He stretched his legs out and linked his hands behind his head. 'What are we going to do about it all?' He turned his head and raised his eyebrows at her.

'You don't seem to be particularly concerned,' she accused with some frustration. 'What you may not understand is that Marion is the most easy-going, loving and lovable person most of the time but just sometimes, when she gets a bee in her bonnet, she can be—*formidable.*'

'Caiti,' he lowered his arms and shoved a hand through his hair with almost savage impatience, 'all this sounds to me as if it's symptomatic of deeper problems that only *they* can sort out. You and I are another matter entirely.'

'She is my cousin, though, so I have to be concerned for her and—'

'No, listen to me,' he ordered roughly. 'Be as concerned as you like for her but all we can do is tell them the truth and offer to be civilised about it if they still want us in the wedding party— I presume we could do that?' he asked with a sardonic quirk of his lips.

'Of course,' she said annoyedly, 'but—'

'Hang on, let me finish. Just don't try and tell me you can push us onto some backburner until after the wedding. If ever,' he added.

'Rob—'

'Caiti, we're married,' he gritted. 'We were married for two days when you took off and disappeared—'

'And you know *why* I did,' she broke in intensely. 'If you'd told me at the time that you wouldn't have slept with me if you'd known I was a virgin, which is admirable behaviour, unless you happen to be the virgin in question!—all of this might have been avoided,' she said bitterly.

'I did marry you,' he pointed out.

'Again, if you'd told me it *suited* you to get married so you could go home to Leicester Downs with a wife, I'd never have done it.'

'Mea culpa,' he drawled. 'How sure are you of those accusations?'

'As sure as I am of anything. I heard you talking to your stepmother, remember?'

'You'd have heard nothing if you hadn't been manning the switchboard that day at Camp Ondine and persistently mixing up calls.' He loosened his tie and undid the top button of his shirt.

'I'm glad that at least you absolve me of deliberately snooping—I thought I was helping out because

you were short-staffed. I'd never handled that kind
of system before.'

'All the same, it was obviously riveting stuff.'

Caiti set her teeth. 'The fact remains I heard someone ask you why on earth you'd married out of the
blue. I heard you reply that you'd made an error of
judgement but it wasn't your custom to seduce vir-
gins and abandon them.'

'And it never crossed your mind I might have used
those terms to fend off my stepmother's almost in-
satiable curiosity?'

'Did you?' she countered. 'You may not remember
this but I think you were about to say something very
similar just after you slept with me.'

'I remember every lovely inch of you and exactly
how you slept with me, as it happens, Caiti.'

She breathed frustratedly. 'That's not the point!
You also told your stepmother a wife was exactly
what you needed to keep your *sister-in-law* off your
back if you were to go home and take over Leicester
Downs while Steve was incapacitated. How do you
think I felt about that? I'll tell you—it made me understand that you *needed* a wife to be able to go
home again. That's when I understood it all.'

'Caiti—'

But she went on as if he hadn't spoken, 'That's
when I realised the difference between *needing* a
wife—and that's all you ever said, Rob—and falling
in *love*.'

He was silent, then, 'All the same, when I suggested we get married, I told you I had a past that should be explained—that was it. My sister-in-law threw me over for my brother, then regretted it. She was the reason I left the station in the first place. But you insisted it was the future that mattered.' He sat forward. 'Perhaps I took the easy way out then, or perhaps I misjudged you.'

'What does that mean?' she whispered.

He looked sombrely through the dark park. 'It never really crossed my mind that you were a virgin. Just as it didn't cross my mind that the facts of my past would prove so...catastrophic for you, or that you'd even get to know them, for that matter.' He paused and shoved his hands in his pockets irritably. 'This is no excuse but I was under a lot of pressure at the time.'

She gestured, palms out. 'I do understand that...well...it all blew up so suddenly for you, but...' She licked a stray tear off her lip.

She had, she recalled all too clearly, insisted that Rob's past didn't mean a thing to her and she didn't want to know about it. Her joy at his proposal and the whirlwind wedding that had followed had been so great, she'd floated through it all a foot off the ground.

Now she had to acknowledge that not only had he misread her, but she'd also misread herself. She'd put off falling madly in love with a man until she was twenty-one but had she been as immature and naive about it as a seventeen-year-old? Was that what he was implying—that he hadn't expected her to act so…immaturely?

Hang on, though, she thought, does the blame all hang with me? A past that could be ignored was one thing, provided you took into account the marks it may have left. But Rob's past was inevitably bound up with his present, wasn't it? The woman who had caused it all was still his sister-in-law, still living in his home, still married to his brother.

'Why haven't you started divorce proceedings?' she asked in a clogged voice.

'Caiti, there has to be a way we can—'

'Resolve our differences?' she suggested with audible irony and added, 'One thing is for sure, we can't go on like this. Something needs to be finalised.'

'As in getting back together?'

She shook her head.

He went still. 'You want a divorce? Why?'

'Rob—'

'So you can get married again?' he suggested coolly.

Caiti moved restlessly. 'That's none of your business.'

'Yes it is. Who is he?'

She got up abruptly and walked down to the water's edge. Of course there was no one, but what had changed? If she'd been vulnerable to Rob at the time, how much more vulnerable would she be if he knew that she'd been unable even to think of another man since marrying him? So, would it provide her with a bit of armour to have him think there was another man in her life?

No, she thought. I have every good reason for what I did and for not going back to him without manufacturing one!—only to find, as she turned away from the water, that he was right behind her. Not only that but she also found herself perpetuating the myth of another man in her life without having to say a word on the subject...

'I wonder if he makes you feel the way I used to,' he said softly, and cupped her shoulders.

She tried to break free but he wouldn't let her. She'd never been any match for him strength-wise but what panicked her was the fact that she was still so defenceless against his proximity. The crisp cotton of his shirt might be hiding the sleek muscles of his shoulders and taut diaphragm but she was as aware of them as she ever had been.

Nothing was hiding the lines of his face, the way his hair fell or the strength of his hands. And she knew that, very soon, she'd be unable to hide the sexy impact just breathing in his pure man essence had on her.

'Don't do this, Rob,' she said urgently, trying to break away again. 'It won't solve anything.'

'Won't it?' He drew her closer. 'Does he know about the music?'

Her lips parted.

'Remember how we slept in the next morning and

you got dressed in such a hurry you forgot your panties?'

A nerve started to hammer at the base of her throat and colour flooded her cheeks.

'I told you,' he traced her mouth with his thumb, 'it was fine with me—what more could I ask for than you floating around all day panty-less?'

She swallowed convulsively.

'Remember the reading room, Caiti?'

Her lashes sank again beneath the weight of memories as vivid as if they'd happened yesterday, and his hands moved downwards to cup her derrière— he'd commented on it at their very first meeting, she recalled, and had never failed to be fascinated by it.

'Rob, no,' she breathed, and tried to jerk away.

Then they both froze as a flashlight played over them and a strange voice said, 'Any problems here, sir? Ma'am?'

They turned to see two officers of the law, all shining belts, boots, buckles, handcuffs and two shades of sharply pressed blue uniform, standing behind them.

Rob released her and swore beneath his breath. 'No, everything is fine, thank you, officers.'

'Ma'am?' one of them enquired of Caiti.

'Uh…he's right. It was just a little disagreement. I'm…I'm fine. Really.'

'All right, we might just take your names to be on the safe side, though, and any problems, you just give us a call, ma'am.'

*   *   *

It wasn't until they were back in the Range Rover that Rob said through his teeth, 'I don't believe it!' He gripped the steering wheel.

'Believe me,' Caiti was starting to see the funny side to it, 'anything could happen in the next two weeks. We've entered a very delicate period known as the PWIP.'

He cast her a grim look. 'The *what*?'

'The Pre-Wedding Insanity Period. Haven't you ever heard of it?' she asked innocently. 'It's a well-known phenomenon but I must say even I had no idea it could get so—seriously insane.'

For a long moment his eyes didn't change, then the grimness softened. 'Oh, Caiti,' he said barely audibly, 'I've missed you.'

She trembled because it would be the easiest, most lovely thing in the world to melt into his arms; it was what her whole body yearned for, it was like coming alive again to sensations she remembered so well as if, suddenly, the barren months no longer existed.

She closed her eyes and felt him reach for the tie holding back her hair, take it off and throw it into the back seat. Her hair tumbled down around her shoulders and he smoothed it with his fingers, and tucked it behind her ears. Then those fingers trailed a path of intimacy down her slender neck towards the buttons of her shirt.

Suddenly they were entwined in each other's arms and he was kissing her throat, her mouth and touching her breasts in their twin cups of lacy bra. What was more, she was revelling in it—the feel of his hard fingers against her soft flesh, the taste of him, the warmth and bulk of him—until once again they were bathed in light.

They drew apart abruptly, Rob swearing audibly this time, but it was the headlights of a car reversing out of a space close to them. All the same Caiti shrank in her seat and started doing up her blouse with unsteady fingers.

'I'm jinxed,' he said bitterly as she ran her fingers through her hair and attempted to straighten her collar.

'If it had been the police they may have been reassured about your intentions towards me,' she said breathlessly.

He switched the engine on. 'If it had been the police,' he said with a wry half-smile, 'we could have found ourselves charged with indecent behaviour in a public place.'

She took a breath. 'What about—irrational behaviour in the circumstances?'

He put the car into gear and reversed out of the parking slot. 'Caiti—'

'Where are we going?' she broke in huskily.

'I don't know. Where would you like to go?'

'Home.'

'Look,' he said, 'there was nothing indecent about it. It was simply a play on words. As for irrational—'

'Rob, *please*,' she said, 'I can't take any more at

the moment. I'm overloaded, I'm exhausted and I just can't think straight.'

He drove a couple of blocks in silence, then, 'Who is he?'

'Who?' she asked stupidly.

'The man you want to divorce me for.'

She refused to answer and reached over into the back seat for her hair tie.

'He doesn't seem to be doing a great job at satisfying you physically—going for a meeting of minds this time, Caiti?'

He nosed the Range Rover into the kerb outside Marion's house and turned to her with a question in his eyes.

When she didn't respond, he added with soft but lethal satire, 'Now, a girl like you should think twice about that. You may have been a virgin but you caught on pretty damn quick.'

Caiti took a huge breath, spoke some very rapid French as she flung her door open and exited the vehicle like a cork out of a bottle. She then looked in at him and repeated what she'd said in English— *'I would rather consort with a snake than you, Rob Leicester'!*

'So much for being civilised,' he drawled. 'Listen, just tell Marion about us, Caiti,' he added. 'Because I intend to tell Derek tomorrow.' He put the car into gear and drove off.

Caiti stood on the pavement and watched his tail-lights until they were out of sight. Then she turned to the house. It was in darkness and there was no car in the carport—Marion was obviously still out.

Not sure whether to be relieved or not, she climbed the steps and rubbed her face wearily as she sank down into a chair on the veranda. It was a cloudy night and the humidity of the tropics, even in May, lay in the air. Cicadas shrilled and the perfume of a flowering shrub wafted up to her on an errant breath of air.

She closed her eyes and remembered another scent on the air—salt.

It had been a wild, stormy day, the day she'd left Rob Leicester. A day that had matched her emotions.

For forty-eight hours she'd been on an incredible high, after their simple, rushed wedding with only the camp staff in attendance and Rob's off-sider, Clint Walker, both best man and giving away the bride. A marriage celebrant had been brought to Camp Ondine from Cairns.

She'd worn her favourite colour, lavender, a long, filmy dress and threaded sparkly silver beads through her hair. He'd worn his crisp white shirt and trousers, and had put a chased silver ring, studded with diamonds, on her finger.

Two days later, they had been due to leave Camp Ondine for Leicester Downs. Because of their impending departure and because of the amount of time Rob had spent at his brother's bedside, the camp had been in some disarray. So she'd offered to man the reception desk. That was when she'd got her telephone lines mixed up, and had frozen to hear a strange woman enquiring who on earth Rob had married out of the blue and why.

His reply had been exactly as she'd previously reminded him, although as she sat on Marion's veranda in the darkness she realised there was one detail she'd left out. His stepmother, not that she knew who it was at the time, had also said that his father was absolutely furious…

It had been like a blow in the solar plexus. She'd simply left the desk, gone briefly to her cabin then wandered down to the beach, completely shell-shocked.

That was where he'd found her an hour or so later, sitting on a bench watching the wild grey sea, her back to the stinging sand blown up by the wind.

She had a baseball cap on with her hair pulled through the back and dark glasses. A loose white linen blouse over denim shorts flapped in the breeze and her feet were bare.

As he moved round to face her, he saw that she was staring down at her wedding ring—sitting in the palm of her hand.

'Caiti?' He frowned.

She jumped, and the ring fell onto the beach.

He bent down and picked it up. 'What?'

Her throat worked. 'Rob, who were you talking to earlier? On the phone?'

His gaze narrowed and he went still. 'My stepmother—why?'

'I h-heard it all,' she said jerkily. 'I got the lines mixed up then couldn't…stop listening. Is that really why you married me? Because I was a virgin you couldn't just abandon?'

'Caiti, you seem to forget you have no one. Your parents—'

'That's beside the point, Rob; I need to know everything! I need to know if I'm some sort of protective armour against your sister-in-law, whoever she is! Tell me about her.' A couple of tears slid beneath the rim of her sunglasses but she ignored them.

'You said none of this mattered,' he pointed out grimly, and slipped the ring into his shirt pocket.

'I said that because I didn't realise—' she stopped and shivered suddenly, '—it might be more a practical thing for you to do—marry me at this crucial point in time, in other words—than anything else. Who is she, Rob?'

A nerve flickered in his jaw but he said evenly, 'We were lovers once. Then she met my brother, Steve, and appeared to fall madly for him. What I didn't realise when *they* married was that she wanted to have her cake and eat it.'

Caiti stared at him. 'So she still—wants you? How very uncomfortable for you.'

He looked over her shoulder into the distance. 'Actually, I'm more concerned for Steve,' he said finally and his voice was so cold, Caiti shivered again. However, if she thought her world had fallen apart before, now it really did, as he added pointedly, 'Who is fighting for his life as we speak.'

She closed her eyes and inhaled deeply. 'So this was just a marriage of convenience for you?'

'Caiti,' he said roughly, 'how "convenient" does it feel when you're in my arms, in my bed?'

She shot up off the bench. 'But would you have asked me to *marry* you if all this hadn't happened? Would you have slept with me in the first place if you'd known I was a virgin?'

That nerve flickered in his jaw again. 'Probably not, but—'

'Then that's what it is,' she insisted. 'You suddenly found yourself lumbered with an ex-virgin and a whole lot of awkward baggage at home—and do you know what?' Her eyes widened as it hit her. 'I don't think you actually want to be in love with me or anyone, Rob Leicester.'

'Why the hell not?'

'Love didn't work for you once, why should it again? Isn't that why you have these *walls* I sensed in your heart but foolishly decided to ignore?'

He reached out swiftly and took her sunglasses off. Her eyes were wet but terribly accusing.

He sighed suddenly, threaded her glasses on top of her cap and shoved his hands into his pockets. 'If there are any walls, Caiti, I have every intention of giving our marriage my best shot. You must admit we're really good together in so many ways—'

'No, Rob,' she broke in out of a throat that hurt.

'We're good in bed but that's been about it. You see, I've just realised I don't know anything about you. It…it's been… Our time together has been like living in a time capsule!'

'And what do you propose to do about that?' he drawled, his eyes hardening.

'I…' she licked her lips '…just don't think I can go on.'

'OK.' He reached into his shirt pocket, picked up her hand and laid her wedding ring in it. 'When you work out how we can *not* go on, since we are now legally married, let me know, won't you?' And he turned away to stride back up the beach towards the camp.

Caiti stared down at her wedding ring, and knew only one thing. To let Rob Leicester go on hurting her would be insane…

She came out of her reverie on Marion's veranda, and wondered painfully if she'd done the right thing that far-off day at Camp Ondine.

Should she have made allowances for the fact that they both could be hot-tempered? Should she have thought a bit longer and harder before slipping unseen aboard the barge that arrived later that afternoon with supplies for the camp, and hitching a ride back to Cairns?

Should she at least, having made that kind of statement, have let Rob come to her with any suggestions rather than disappearing out of his life?

At the time she'd been so shattered and hurt it had been the only thing she'd been capable of doing, but now she was forced to wonder.

Because three little words—*I've missed you*—had seen her fall back into his arms as if she'd never left them.

CHAPTER FIVE

Marion still hadn't come in by the time Caiti went to bed in almost a stupor of exhaustion.

All the same, she slept badly, and when she got up the next morning she had to use foundation to conceal the dark shadows below her eyes.

Marion, on the other hand, as Caiti arrived in the kitchen, appeared to be bright and bouncy as she greeted her cousin and tossed pancakes with gay abandon.

Caiti sat down at the kitchen table and poured herself a glass of orange juice. 'All sorted with Derek?' she queried.

Marion slid the pancakes onto plates and brought them over to the table. 'Yes! Mind you, I had to make a couple of concessions.'

She went back to the stove for the percolator, which was bubbling gently and filling the kitchen with the lovely aroma of freshly ground coffee.

'Such as?'

Marion sat down and looked rueful. 'I agreed to be much more conciliatory towards his mother.'

Caiti buttered her pancake. 'Is that so hard to do?'

Marion shrugged. 'I guess not. I've fought most of the battles to do with the wedding and when I come to think of it, there is one thing Mrs Handy has in common with me. She's all for us getting married. I think she'd have liked us to do the deed about six months after we met.'

'She must approve of you, then.'

'As much as she approves of anything.' Marion wrinkled her nose. 'When you get to meet her you'll understand what I mean. She's— I think she's the most critical, suspicious person I've ever met. But she is his mother so I'll just have to live with it.'

Caiti drizzled honey onto her pancake. 'What's the other concession?'

Marion flicked a little glance heavenwards then said with due solemnity, 'I have given my word that I will put my best foot forward with Rob Leicester— no more snide remarks et cetera.'

Caiti cut her pancake into quarters and stared down at it for a long moment, knowing that trying to eat it would choke her.

'Marion,' she heard herself say as if in the distance, 'there's something I have to tell you.'

'Fire away!' Marion poured two cups of coffee and pushed one towards Caiti.

'Thanks.' She hesitated as she tried to think of a way to minimise the impact of her news but there was none. 'Rob Leicester and I are married.'

For a moment it didn't sink in. Then Marion gasped and spluttered. '*Caiti!* You're not serious?'

Caiti closed her eyes and gestured helplessly.

'Why didn't you tell me this yesterday?'

'I got such a shock, I couldn't think straight. As a matter of fact, I bumped into him at the airport.'

'But…what went wrong?'

Caiti studied her hands then raised her eyes to her cousin. 'I discovered it was a marriage of convenience for him.' She moved her shoulders restlessly. 'I should have realised it but I didn't and it came as such a shock, I left him.'

Marion still looked absolutely stunned. 'How long ago was this?'

'Eighteen months.'

'So I was right about the man all the time!'

'No. Marion, no!' Caiti said desperately. 'Look, there was no way you could have known and it's…it's really no reason why we can't proceed as planned. I'm sure Rob and I can be…um…civilised about it but I just couldn't hide it from you any longer. It was bound to come out sooner or later.'

'There's every reason not to proceed as planned,' Marion said grimly. 'Derek will just to have to find someone else. Oh, you poor thing! Tell me all about it.'

Caiti bit her lip but there was no way to evade at least a limited version of what had happened. When she finished, Marion stared at her wordlessly for a long moment.

Then she struck at the heart of the matter unerringly. 'Are you still in love with him?'

Caiti winced. 'I don't know. I thought I'd put it all behind me.' She gestured. 'I probably have, it was just the shock of bumping into him so unexpectedly yesterday that brought, well, some of it back.'

Marion narrowed her eyes. 'What about him?'

Caiti blinked. 'As in?'

'What does he want to do about your marriage?'

'He wants us to…to try again.'

Marion put her elbow on the table and propped her chin in her hand. 'How would you feel about that?'

Caiti sighed. 'I don't know. Look,' she paused briefly and studied Marion—and could have kicked herself for the new concern shadowing Marion's eyes, 'about the wedding, though, there's no need for you and Derek to be worried. Rob is quite all right really and—'

'Forget the wedding, it's you I'm worried about at the moment,' Marion interrupted. 'You should have written to me. I'd have come home—you had no one!'

Caiti smiled painfully. 'That's exactly why I didn't write to you. And, while I sometimes blame having no one at the time, it might have happened all the same, Marion. He—well, it's so hard to explain but in every other respect he's…I mean, you shouldn't let this colour your feelings about him. And don't—' Caiti hesitated '—forget how much Derek admires Rob, with good cause, I'm sure.'

Marion looked mutinous for a moment then she shrugged. 'I guess I do need to get this into some sort of perspective. All the same…' She paused as they heard a car door close and footsteps coming up the stairs.

It was Derek, and for a moment, as he came into the kitchen, Marion was transformed.

'Hi, darling!' she said. 'This is a lovely surprise!'

Derek kissed her briefly then pulled out a chair and glanced rather awkwardly at Caiti.

He knows, Caiti thought immediately. Rob's been as good as his word...

'Morning,' he said at large and gratefully accepted a cup of coffee from his bride-to-be. 'Uh—we have a bit of a complication. Rob's just rung me.'

It didn't take long for Marion to put two and two together. 'He's confessed!' she said dramatically, causing Caiti to flinch inwardly.

'I wouldn't put it quite like that,' Derek demurred. 'He did explain that, well, after they married and Caiti ran away,' he glanced uneasily at Caiti again, 'he's been desperate to find her. So when I asked him to be my best man and mentioned who one of the bridesmaids was he said nothing about their marriage in case it...well, scared you off again, Caiti.'

Marion narrowed her eyes thoughtfully and studied her cousin rather intently. 'I guess that makes a bit of sense.'

Caiti gripped her fingers together and could think of absolutely nothing to say as she grappled with the unpleasant feeling of being under a microscope.

'What does he suggest now, though?' Marion queried.

Derek cleared his throat. 'He's offered to withdraw from the wedding party if Caiti wishes him to.'

The silence that followed this wasn't golden, it was fraught with tension. Derek had now transferred his attention completely to Marion as if her reaction to this was crucial to him. And Caiti was seized with the sudden dread, as Marion opened her mouth, that her cousin was summarily going to accept Rob's withdrawal, thereby plunging them into even more turmoil.

'There's no need for that,' she said rapidly. 'I'm quite sure Rob and I,' she crossed her fingers below the table, 'can cope. I…well, to be honest, I rather regret running away as I did and, although I don't know how things will work out for us, we do need to…to spend some time together.'

'But things can't be easy between you,' Marion objected.

'I suspect the worst of that is over now,' Caiti lied. 'I haven't told you this yet, Marion, but after you went out last night I got in touch with Rob and we had a long discussion. Nothing got sorted,' she tipped her hand, 'but there's no reason we can't be adult about it.'

Marion looked unconvinced but at the same time curiously assessing as she watched Caiti.

And Derek said, 'He did make another suggestion if Caiti was happy to carry on as planned.'

'What would that be?' Marion asked but almost absent-mindedly as she continued to study Caiti.

'Apparently Camp Ondine is very lightly booked at the moment. So instead of the party we were planning to have here tomorrow night, he's suggested we all go up there for a couple of days.'

This truly got Marion's attention. 'All?' she said blankly.

'Yes,' Derek agreed. 'Mum, Eloise and her boyfriend, you and I—and Caiti, of course. It being a weekend, I presume we're all free?'

'But why?' Marion queried.

Derek shrugged. 'He thought it might bring us all together and I think he's right. As you know, Marion, Mother is fanatical about the preservation of the rainforest, and I think she would really enjoy it up there. I'm sure Eloise and Ritchie would too. You did also say to me once that you would love to see Camp Ondine.'

Marion opened her mouth then closed it.

Under any other circumstances, Caiti thought, it would be a perfect suggestion, but was it diabolically clever of Rob at the same time? The perfect way to get her back at Camp Ondine with all its memories?

'Caiti?' Marion said at last. 'It is something along the lines you suggested yourself but we'd quite understand if you didn't want to go.'

Heaven preserve me from this, Caiti thought a little wildly, but what else is there to do? Look how Marion lit up when Derek arrived unexpectedly, so isn't this a small price to pay towards a smoother, *happier* run up to their wedding?

'I think it would be great,' she said, and added to Derek, 'I'm really looking forward to meeting your mum and your sister.'

His reaction was startlingly plain, relief and genuine pleasure. 'Thanks, Caiti! You're a real pal.'

Nor was it lost on Marion.

After Derek had gone, she too thanked Caiti for pouring oil on troubled waters but asked her penetratingly if she was really sure she could do it.

'There's something,' Caiti said slowly, and truthfully as it happened, 'about Camp Ondine that is unique. I think we'll all find ourselves relaxing. By the way,' she added with a mischievous grin, 'I haven't seen the wedding dress, the bridesmaids' dresses or anything yet!'

So they spent the rest of the day pleasurably going over all the wedding preparations.

Grace Handy was short and wiry with thick grey hair and sharp blue eyes.

She and Caiti met for the first time on Marion's veranda as the wedding party assembled the next morning for the trip to Camp Ondine.

She gave Caiti a thorough going over as they shook hands then remarked, 'You certainly look French!' in a manner that didn't entirely suggest it was a compliment.

'She's only half-French,' Marion supplied with a determined smile, 'but I know what you mean. I just wish I could look *half* as stylish.'

Caiti looked down at her yellow three-quarter cargo trousers, white knit vest-top and yellow sand shoes with a frown. 'What's so stylish about this gear?'

'Darling, it's *you*,' Marion said. 'You would look good in a sack. Come and meet Eloise and Ritchie.'

Eloise was a doe-eyed blonde in her early twenties and Ritchie a hearty young giant with an engaging grin.

'A real pleasure to meet you, Caiti,' he confided and shook her hand with gusto.

Eloise raised a languid eyebrow but said in a friendly enough way, 'Actually we've all been dying to meet you!' Then she spoilt it immediately by adding, 'Any girl who turns her back on Rob Leicester has got to be quite something.'

'Now, Eloise,' Derek admonished, 'we weren't going to mention that, were we?'

'Sorry—just slipped out,' his sister said airily, and they all turned as a four-wheel-drive bus bearing the Camp Ondine logo turned into the drive, and fortunately the awkward moment was lost in the bustle of boarding.

But Caiti was left with several uncomfortable impressions. Derek's mother and sister were not going to be impressed by her on face value but whether it was because of her 'Frenchness', Ritchie's unqualified approval or her background with Rob, she wasn't too sure. Maybe it's all three, she pondered.

Or maybe, she thought suddenly, there are two

camps here. The Handys and the Galloways and never the twain shall meet—no, that's ridiculous! But is it? she wondered. Had Derek inherited his reserve and uncomfortable ways from his mother? A kind of siege mentality? The kind of—*we're as good as anybody*—inferiority complex? Perhaps…

Or is it just me?

Ritchie saved the day during the long drive to the camp. He'd brought along his guitar—he was a gifted musician as well as thoroughly likeable—and he soon had them all singing to while away the miles.

In fact they arrived at Camp Ondine in a lot more unity than they'd set out, although Grace Handy was still bestowing upon Caiti the odd dubious little look.

Rob was there to welcome them, the first time Caiti had set eyes on him since their last eventful meeting. For an instant things got tense again as they greeted each other—was everyone holding their breath? she wondered—but she called on every ounce of poise she possessed. Rob was obviously in laid-back mode so the moment passed with no awkwardness at all.

Marion later confided to Caiti that she was unwittingly impressed with Rob's warm and charismatic welcome.

Clint Walker, Rob's off-sider, was still at Camp Ondine and he greeted Caiti affectionately, enthusiastically and with no trace of embarrassment, causing her to breathe a little easier too.

Then Rob suggested to the party that he give them a guided tour of the camp, after which they might like to do their own thing for the rest of the afternoon before joining up for drinks and a barbecue around the pool.

Everyone agreed it sounded like heaven, and Caiti trotted along obediently although she knew Camp Ondine like the back of her hand.

Some of her composure wore off, however, when she discovered that she was allotted her same cabin.

'I hope you're not still next door?' she enquired frostily.

'I am. There is still a wall between us and you're welcome to lock your door.'

'I will,' she said then felt foolish, so she tossed her head.

He looked amused. 'Talk about closing the stable door after the horse has bolted.'

She gritted her teeth.

'Maybe you need a break, Caiti,' he added softly. And he strolled down the veranda steps and out of sight, whistling softly.

She closed herself in and leant against the door, with the knowledge seeping through her that she should never have done this to herself. There were too many memories to cope with.

There was the simple fact, for one thing, that she'd grown to love Camp Ondine almost like a home. She'd even thought of suggesting to Rob once that it would be a marvellous setting in all its wild splen-

dour for some cultural events that she could special-
ise in organising. Concerts, perhaps, or…

Stop it, she advised herself. Has he changed?

It was a question she couldn't answer and tension
saw her succumb to sheer weariness.

There was no wake-up call for her this time, no
mysterious pick-me-up, but by the time Marion
knocked on her door she'd had a shower and was
wondering what to wear.

Marion, in fact, surprised her. She wore an attractive and slimming long black dress with one bare
shoulder, her hair was swept over to the other side
and in her exposed ear she wore a dangly earring
with red and yellow enamelled flowers.

'Wow!' Caiti saluted her. 'You look wonderful.'

Marion beamed. 'It's actually part of my honeymoon gear but it seemed a sin not to break it out for
a place like this. What are you wearing?'

'Hadn't thought. What do you reckon? I haven't
unpacked properly yet.'

Marion tut-tutted and rifled through Caiti's bag.
'This,' she said definitely, and brought out a pair of
white hipster trousers and a short smoky-grey knit
top with tiny pearls sewn on it.

'Marion,' Caiti said laughingly, 'your mother-in-
law already suspects me of—heaven knows what! If
I go around flashing my navel—'

'She's not my mother-in-law yet, and with your
figure it's a sin not to wear them. They're so in! Have
you any idea how I would love to be able to wear

these kinds of clothes?' she asked dramatically and added, 'Why did you pack them if you didn't intend to wear them?'

'I didn't pack them for Camp Ondine. I never got around to *unpacking* them at your place and I just threw some things into this bag on top of them to bring up here.'

'OK, but since you brought them, it's a shame not to wear them! He's quite something, isn't he?'

It was a *non sequitur* but Caiti understood immediately. 'I guess so,' she murmured and sat down at the dresser to brush her hair.

'For instance,' Marion went on, 'despite what I've been *told* to do, I came here prepared to hate him but it didn't happen.'

'I tried to tell you he was all right.'

'Hmm…' Marion shrugged. 'To be honest, I found myself thinking you two were well-suited.'

Caiti turned on the stool to frown at her cousin. 'You couldn't possibly make that judgement so quickly! You've only just met him.'

'On the contrary, I've just spent a while with him, having a chat.'

Caiti's eyes widened. 'What about? Us? I mean, Rob and me?'

'Caiti,' Marion sat down on the edge of the bed, 'Rob Leicester seems to be playing such a significant part in our lives at the moment, I thought it would be only fair and square to tell him where I stood. Not only on your account but also on Derek's.'

Caiti stared at her helplessly while she turned her brush over and over in her hands.

Marion got up and came over to the dresser. 'We didn't go into any real details but I told him how much you meant to me and how I hated to see you hurt. He said he quite understood, and, hard though it may be for me to accept, he does have your best interests at heart. I—' she paused '—I believed him.'

'Would you...?' Caiti stopped and cleared her throat. 'Would you marry a man who had your best interests at heart, Marion?'

Marion hesitated. 'I know what you mean but you could do a lot worse. The point is, he's not what I thought he would be and perhaps you should, well, give him a decent hearing. OK. No more sermonising but it might give you a bit of peace of mind to know I'm not hating his guts any more!'

Despite herself, Caiti had to smile.

Marion observed it and kissed her lightly on top of her head. 'I'll leave you to get dressed but don't be long. I intend both ''Galloway gals'' to sock it to them tonight!'

Caiti watched her go but then prudently decided to wear a top that did not expose her navel.

CHAPTER SIX

THE 'other' Galloway gal apparently surprised her fiancé as well as her cousin.

In deference to Grace Handy's sensibilities, Eloise and her boyfriend as well as Derek and Marion had all been given their own private cabins. Thus it was that, whatever transpired later in the evening, Derek did not behold his bride-to-be looking *trés chic* in her new black dress, until they all met at the barbecue area.

For a moment he looked stunned. So did his mother.

Then he said, sounding as if he'd been conspired against, 'I've never seen that dress before, Marion!'

How like a man, Caiti thought again. How like a husband... Oh, dear, she thought next, what does that mean?

But Marion appeared oblivious to any innuendoes as she twirled so her skirt belled out. 'Don't you like it?' she teased.

'It's...' Derek struggled for words.

'I think it's stunning,' Ritchie said into the pause and looked to Eloise for agreement.

'So do I,' Rob put in, in the act of opening a bottle of champagne. 'In fact I think you all look stunning.'

His gaze encompassed Eloise, Grace Handy and finally Caiti herself, on whom it lingered briefly with something she couldn't identify in his eyes, until he turned to the drinks trolley and poured the champagne.

'Actually,' he continued, handing out glasses, 'it calls for a toast, Derek, don't you think?'

'I... Yes, of course! To all our lovely ladies!' Derek raised his glass gallantly.

There was an expectant little pause.

'But—my fiancée in particular!' he added.

Everyone put their glasses down to clap, and for some reason Caiti found herself breathing a little easier.

There were no more hitches, imagined or otherwise, for the rest of the evening. A tribute to Rob, Ritchie and Marion, Caiti decided when the party finally broke up. Somehow they'd loosened everyone up although Derek's mother was still casting Caiti the odd, suspicious little look.

Then Grace yawned and excused herself, Eloise and Ritchie drifted away with Marion and Derek following not much later, leaving Caiti and Rob alone. Caiti was in a private little reverie and not really aware of it until Rob spoke.

'A successful evening?'

The barbecue had burned down but the braziers were still flaming against the dark, velvety sky.

She came out of her reverie, suddenly realising they were alone as she looked around. 'Yes. Well, I guess you have all sorts of activities planned for to-morrow?'

'I thought we might go out to the Hope Isles if the weather holds.'

'Great.' Caiti forced herself to sound enthusiastic then frowned. 'Don't you have guests this weekend?'

'Nope. Not one.'

'How come?'

He smiled idly. 'Is that the old tour guide in you coming to the fore?'

'I… It's just…we always had to book Camp Ondine well in advance, it was so popular.'

'It still is but we happened to have a rare cancellation.'

Caiti sank back and studied him as he relaxed in a lounger. 'For a moment I wondered if you were going out of business.'

'Thank you for your concern,' he murmured.

'Thank you also,' she gestured a little stiffly, 'for thinking of this. Marion is—like a new person.'

'My pleasure.'

'Well,' she got up, 'I'll go to bed.'

'Why don't you?'

But there was something so lazily insolent in the way he said it, it gave her pause.

'Look,' she began evenly, 'don't spoil what has been a very nice gesture—'

'Nice gesture be damned.'

'What…what do you mean?'

He shrugged. 'It was the only way I could think of to get you back here, Caiti.'

She gasped.

He stood up and loomed over her but made no attempt to touch her. 'You probably think you know the baser side of me rather well,' he said wryly and added, 'In this case you're right. Why do you think you've got the same cabin?'

'*Why?*'

He smiled. 'I wanted to arouse as many memories as I could. That's why we're going out to Hope tomorrow.'

'That's diabolical,' she got out. 'Don't you think it was hard enough to come back here in any event but...?' She stopped abruptly.

'Hard? Why?'

She swallowed.

'Has it been that hard to forget me, Caiti?' he asked.

Her eyes were huge—and trapped. He put his fingers very lightly on her throat, and she shivered but was unable to move away.

'You see,' he continued barely audibly, 'if there's any possibility of me making amends, at the very least, I need to know that.'

'So we can continue our marriage of *convenience*, Rob?'

He hesitated then dropped his hand. 'Could we not move on at least one step from that?'

'To the other women in your life?' she suggested

with bitter irony. 'Yes, we could move on a step but not right now.'

He raised an eyebrow. 'Tired? You used to have a lot more energy.'

'I'm—not in the right frame of mind. And insulting me is not likely to get me into the right frame of mind. For your further information,' she added with a lethal kind of sweetness, 'no, I am not tired at all! What do you suggest we do about that—other than the obvious?' She eyed him sardonically.

'Brew ourselves a cup of coffee and I could show you the plans for Camp Caiti.'

'Camp Caiti?' She blinked at him.

'Yes, Caiti, as in short for Caitlin.'

'You…you've named a camp after me?'

He nodded.

'But why?' She was astounded.

'It's a lovely spot that reminded me of you,' he said as her expression changed. 'Come and have a look.'

On the wall of his office there was a blown-up aerial photo of a wilderness camp on a rocky river bank. Inset were smaller photos, a map of the Kimberly, West Australia, coastline, and quite clearly, in one corner, in cursive script on a curved banner was the legend: Camp Caiti.

Caiti wrapped her hands around a mug of coffee and stared at the photo bemusedly.

Not that there was a lot of camp to see—the amenities were quite limited—but inland, behind the camp, there was a water-lily-filled lagoon of unusual beauty, plenty of paper-bark gums, flowering bushes and creepers and some exotic palms she didn't recognise.

The river itself wound between low, rocky and green banks often crowned with the palms she didn't recognise either, from its mouth in a huge bay to a series of rocky pools and waterfalls where it continued inland behind this unnavigable barrier.

'This,' Rob laid his forefinger in the area below the waterfalls, 'is where the barramundi wait for the monsoon season, when the level of the river rises, so they can get upstream to spawn in the fresh water. But they're also found throughout the river.'

'So do you fish from the banks?'

'You can, from the rock walls, but it's mostly done by dinghy. You wouldn't want to fish from the banks lower down the river because of the crocodiles. Ever caught a barramundi?'

She shook her head. 'I believe it's very exciting.'

'It is. They fight like crazy.'

'I'd love to try it,' she said enthusiastically then frowned. 'How will you get the guests in? This is seriously remote!'

'By float plane from Kununurra.'

'So, I imagine it's not going to be cheap either?'

'You imagine right. Everything has to be flown in. But there are a lot of men keen for the ultimate barra-fishing adventure.'

'You do obviously have a golden touch, Rob. But—I still can't believe you named it after me.'

He pulled out a chair for her and sat down across an untidy desk from her. 'It's an unusual enough name for it to be catchy.'

She grimaced. 'There you go.'

'But you're an unusual enough person, Caiti Galloway.'

She glanced at him and wondered what he would say if she told him that she hadn't felt particularly 'unusual' for a while—eighteen months in fact.

Then he changed the subject completely. 'Do you think we're going to get Marion and Derek to the altar?'

She looked alarmed. 'Why not? Do you know something I don't?'

He said pensively, 'They've been together a long time.'

'Surely…surely that's a plus?'

'Well, I sometimes wonder if it's not putting the cart before the horse, these extended relationships, then all this fuss about getting married. And I can't help wondering if this is the real, underlying problem we have here.'

Caiti's mouth fell open. She closed it and said, 'But a wedding is, well, *usually* a bit of fuss, yes. And perhaps it is more important to a woman, that big day, but even for a man surely it's a ceremonial formalising of your love—wouldn't you say?'

'Or the clanging shut of the prison door,' he returned softly.

Caiti gasped. 'You don't...don't you believe in marriage? Or don't you believe in love matches?' she added pointedly.

As a verbal dart, it bounced off him harmlessly. 'It's just that I've seen this happen a few times, couples living together for extended periods then not able to take the final step.'

'They weren't living together,' Caiti said at last, the only, and admittedly feeble, thing she could come up with.

He smiled unamusedly. 'As good as.'

'I hope you're wrong in this case,' she said devoutly, 'but...' She paused and frowned at him. 'Would you like to explain a bit more?'

'Maybe,' he said slowly, 'Derek has had it all on a platter for so long, he's reluctant to change the status quo?'

'That sounds very cynical, Rob.'

He gestured.

'What about their way of doing things being preferable to marrying in haste and repenting at leisure?'

This time her dart found its mark. His mouth hardened.

'Is that what you feel you did?'

'Yes. But I also feel I got conned into it.'

Their gazes clashed then he got up and came round the desk to sit on the corner facing her. 'You know,

Caiti,' he said, 'you can continue to feel bitterly righteous about me or you could take another approach.'

She gasped. 'Bitterly righteous! That's—'

'That's how it looks,' he drawled and stuck his thumbs into his belt. 'But if you were to try and put that aside, you might find something quite different.'

And then have to pick up the pieces again?—it flashed through her mind.

'It's up to you.' He stood up.

They were very close, close enough for her to breathe in the pure male essence of Rob Leicester, to examine the lines and planes of his face and the aura of a man who had seen and done a lot but would never beg her to listen to him…

She found that frightening, she realised. Not that she wanted him on his knees, far from it, but the fear that some things about him would always be a closed book to her, as they always had, was still very real in her.

She dropped her eyes away from his and ran her fingers through her hair, spreading it over her shoulders like a rough black silk cloak—in a metaphorical gesture of seeking some shelter.

'I'll think about it.' She looked up at him.

He stared at her shining cloak of hair and a muscle flickered in his jaw.

She tensed but he did nothing. Yet the very air between them was threaded with an almost overpowering awareness of each other, and the memories of being in each other's arms.

Caiti took a ragged breath, and put a hand to her lips. There might always be things she didn't know about this man but he knew her in the most biblical sense. He knew exactly what drove her wild with desire but he also knew her favourite foods, her fears, phobias and foibles.

Worst of all, though, he was still capable of making her want him in a way that was causing that special, pleasurable ache to build deep within her and send a host of thrilling sensations through her veins…

'Think about what?' he said softly. 'That husky little sound you used to make when you came? The way you once begged me not to let you go or you'd fall off the planet? The way you used to adore being kissed from head to toe,' his gaze swept down her body, 'and all stops in between?'

She closed her eyes in disbelief as a rush of colour stained her cheeks.

'That's how close we were, Caiti.'

She opened her eyes to see that he was watching her with a patently ironic expression.

'N-no,' she cleared her throat, 'that's you being as…as mean and nasty as I always knew you could be.'

'What was mean and nasty about it at the time?' he queried mockingly.

'I…mean…what I mean…bringing it up like that is—'

'Hitting below the belt like a real bastard?' he supplied, and lifted a suddenly amused eyebrow. 'In more ways than one, perhaps. Or,' he paused, 'simply telling it the way it was?'

She stared at him, and did the only thing possible. She turned on her heel and ran away from him.

'This is bliss!' Marion pronounced as she and Caiti sunbaked on a pale sandy beach.

Caiti had been spared the Hope Isles because a twenty-knot south-easterly had got up overnight and would have made the trip out too uncomfortable. She hadn't been spared a change of venue for the day's proceedings, though, to a secluded bay fringed with casuarinas and cotton woods and lapped by clear turquoise waters.

The rest of the party were fossicking along the beach or splashing in the water.

No, it's not, it's sheer hell, Caiti replied in her mind.

She sat up and eyed Derek, who was examining some rocks near by. Was he, she wondered, viewing this forthcoming marriage as the clanging of the prison door on him? Did it take a man to understand a man?

'Penny for them?' Marion said gaily as she rubbed more suncream on her arms and legs. She was looking colourful in a white swimsuit splashed with jungle flowers.

'I'm…thinking of the first time I came here,' Caiti

improvised. And she related the story of the French vegetarians.

Marion giggled but said loyally, 'That's not very common, surely?'

Caiti grimaced. 'I later found out they belonged to a vegetarian club back in France. That's why they were travelling together.' She turned over and lay on her stomach, mainly to block the view of Rob, who'd strolled into sight down the beach and joined Derek, but seeing the two men together activated a thought.

She sifted some sand through her fingers and said in a lowered voice to Marion, 'Does Derek know Rob's brother Steve?'

'He's met him a few times, that's all, but it was enough for him to form the opinion that Rob and Steve aren't close. Apparently they got split up when their parents divorced—did you know about that?'

'I—well, I knew Rob had a stepmother,'

'Steve stayed with his father apparently,' Marion said. 'Then Rob went back years later and Derek got the impression it wasn't an easy transition for all concerned, and to complicate matters, their father married a much younger woman and they have a daughter.'

Caiti blinked.

'See,' Marion drew a meaningless squiggle in the sand, 'apparently the Leicester family are a bit larger than life, very rich, and rather colourful.'

'Oh.'

Marion frowned. 'Didn't you know *any* of this at the time?'

'No, but that was partly my fault. So Derek has never mentioned anything about Steve's wife?'

'The one who had Rob first then changed her mind, only to change it again?' Marion looked at Caiti soberly. 'No, I wouldn't have known about it if you hadn't told me but that could be all over and done with now, Caiti. One thing I do know is, she's still with Steve.'

Caiti sifted more sand then stood up suddenly. Her bikini—hot pink with white piping—was revealed as she drew off a diagonally white and pink striped sarong. 'Let's have a swim!'

Lunch on the beach started out pleasantly.

Grace Handy was in her seventh heaven over the unspoiled surroundings. Eloise and Ritchie had not only swum but also played cricket with whomever they could rope in and, causing Caiti to tell herself she was worrying needlessly, Derek and Marion had disappeared around the headland for rather a long time.

And she had started to unpack the picnic lunch more for something to do than because she felt housewifely. Unfortunately, Rob broke off his participation in the cricket to help when he'd noticed what she was doing.

'*Déjà vu?*' he queried as he snapped the folding

table's legs into position and set up some canvas stools.

She glinted him a quick, cool glance—and laid out three salads in yellow bowls.

He eased the lids off dishes of cold chicken and ham carved from the bone.

Almost by reflex, Caiti continued setting out the picnic even to expertly fluffing out colourful paper napkins and putting them in the wine glasses as if the party were actual paying guests. Last of all, Rob placed a small pot of dried flowers in the centre of the table.

'There.' He stepped back. 'Still a pretty good team despite our dubious beginning.'

She eyed the table then looked up at him to see he was eyeing her. She'd knotted her sarong around her, and her hair was in one thick plait, whereas his was tousled and he wore nothing but a pair of maroon shorts.

'Yes,' she said tonelessly. 'I'll just call the faithful to the lunch. Even as good a team as we are, there are still ants, flies and stray breezes to take into account.'

'Not to mention our personal devils.'

Her gaze flew back to his but he merely smiled unamusedly.

She swallowed and Derek and Marion strolled up, Marion expressing delight at the elegant presentation of lunch.

'I had heard you do things very well up here, Rob,'

Grace Handy remarked, also arriving and claiming a canvas stool. 'I'm now convinced of it.'

'Thank you, Grace,' Rob responded as he opened a bottle of wine. 'I must say I always used to count on Caiti to make a very decorative addition to any proceedings up here. She really used to liven things up.'

'I can imagine,' Grace offered with a tinge of malice.

'Mother,' Derek warned.

Grace shrugged and at Rob's gesture, began to help herself. Caiti grimaced inwardly. The battle to win over Derek's mother would seem to be a long way from won.

But Eloise and Ritchie had arrived in time to hear Grace's remark, and Ritchie said humorously, 'I'm sure Caiti could liven up any occasion.'

Eloise planted her hands on her hips and took exception. 'You men!'

'You're right, Eloise, I was only doing my job.' Caiti said calmly.

'Well,' Marion helped herself and sat down, 'Caiti obviously inherited her French mother's chic style as well as being one of the most hardworking and nicest people I know.'

So put that in your pipe and smoke it, was the unspoken and slightly irrational inference that came over loud and clear, causing Caiti to flinch inwardly, and dig really deep to rescue the situation.

'Being half-French can have its disadvantages,'

she said ruefully. 'I once caused all kinds of chaos because I told my boss he was an arrogant pig, amongst other things, in French,' she paused and grimaced at an unpleasant memory, 'not realising that his wife, who was with him at the time, understood every word.'

'What kind of a job would that have been?' Grace asked.

'Governess to a set of twins from hell during the school holidays once. He was their father.'

'And he hadn't, by any chance, made a pass at you?' Grace enquired, getting to the heart of the matter with an unerring instinct that took Caiti's breath away for a moment.

'He…' She paused and subjected Grace Handy to a dangerous lavender gaze. 'Yes, he had. So what?'

Grace shrugged. 'Men have a habit of making fools of themselves over certain women.'

Caiti looked down at her plate, upon which she had just heaped potato salad, green salad and some ham. And with a flick of her wrist she tipped the plate over so it all slid onto the sand almost at Grace's feet. 'Take that, you old bat,' she said in French, dumped the plate on the table and marched away.

About a minute later, she broke into a run and sprinted along the damp, firm sand at the edge of the water until she was out of sight of the lunch party around the headland. That was where Rob caught up with her.

'Go away!' she yelled at him, speeding up again.

But he caught her all the same and literally man-handled her until she could only subside, panting, in his arms.

'I…hate…you!' she got out between sucking in great breaths of air. 'You started it all. You and your bloody "decorative" tag. You *fuelled* all this non-sense, you always did hold that suspect view of me… You're as bad as Derek's mother, who obviously thinks I ask men to make passes at me!'

'Caiti—'

'I don't want to hear it! Thanks to you I've undone all the good work, all the fences I was desperately trying to mend so Marion could have a pleasant, memorable run up to her wedding. Not to mention,' she paused for breath, 'helping to foster this crazy impression that I'm some *French…floozie!*'

She wrenched her arm free and, so great was her anger and distress, went to slap his face.

He caught her wrist and pinned her arm behind her back. Then he took her chin firmly in his other hand and bent his head to kiss her.

Five minutes later they were sitting on the sand about two feet apart, staring out to sea.

'I can't believe you did that,' Caiti said, and licked her swollen lips.

'Seemed the only way to defuse things.'

'It hasn't defused anything from my point of view.'

He turned his head and looked at her, his eyes

glinting in a way that was purely wicked. 'At least you stopped wanting to knock me out.'

A tinge of colour entered her cheeks. 'It hasn't answered anything, though,' she said stiffly.

He lay back on one elbow. 'Yes, it has. It may have come out in different ways but I think it would be fair to say we were both suffering from serious sexual frustration.'

She turned to him convulsively. 'What did *I* do? And are you saying your urge to insult me was the result of frustration?'

'Undoubtedly.'

'That's…' She gestured and was lost for words.

'As for what you did—nothing. But your tension was almost palpable and the fact that you were not talking to me was obvious.'

Caiti gaped at him. 'That's not true.'

He merely looked at her.

'I have a lot to worry about at the moment,' she said with dignity.

He shrugged. 'Look, I appreciate what you're trying to do for Marion but you can only do so much. Some battles she has to fight for herself. What did you call her?'

'Who?'

'Mrs Handy.'

'An old bat,' Caiti said with relish. Then she sighed dismally. 'Marion warned me about her but I honestly didn't expect her to be so difficult and so…critical. I've never done her—I haven't known her long enough to do her a moment's harm.' She put her hands around her legs and rested her chin on her knees. 'How did you leave them?'

He raised an eyebrow at her.

'Derek, Marion and his mother. Were they having words?'

'No. Ritchie came to the rescue. Apparently Grace has a soft spot for him so when he suggested she might have been a bit hard on you, she gave it some thought then agreed. Which took the wind right out of Marion's sails.'

'If you had a feather you could knock me down with it,' Caiti observed.

'He also gave it out to be understood that his remark had only been meant as a compliment. In fact,' Rob continued, 'I've been deputised to present their apologies to you and to collect you and take you back so you can have some lunch.'

This time Caiti pressed her forehead to her knees as a gurgle of laughter rose to her throat. Then she was laughing helplessly and so was he.

Caiti lay down on the sand and opened her arms wide. 'I think I'm going mad,' she hiccuped, still giggling like a schoolgirl. 'I think I might have flipped. I mean, it's not funny really—we've got over a week to go—but you know what makes it even funnier?' She sat up and looked down at him.

'Tell me.'

She waved her arms again. 'We're in this absolutely marvellous spot, so unspoiled, on the edge of the Great Barrier Reef, there's so much space, light, sea, air, sand—and we're squabbling over nothing really.'

'That strikes you as funny?' He sat up and looked at her wryly.

'Yes. That's why I think I've flipped. It's all so insignificant compared to this it's laughable. Or something like that.' She grinned. 'Anyway, I feel a bit better.'

'Caiti, only you could look at it like that.' He put his arm around her, drawing her down to the sand with him.

'You're agreeing with me that I'm seriously cuckoo if not to say deluded?' she teased.

'Definitely. I'll go one further—delicious and desirable.'

Caiti caught her breath as months rolled away and she was right back in the days when she'd loved Rob Leicester with a kind of joy she'd never known before or since. To the days when they'd laughed together and her personality had bubbled and flowered and, or so she'd thought, he'd loved it.

Then he drew her closer and his mouth came down hard on hers again.

Heat and desire flooded through her. The feel of his hard, muscled chest against her breasts, his legs entwined with hers, excited her to writhe in his arms. And when he undid her sarong and unclipped her bikini top she was as aroused as only he could make her, with her nipples aching as they became taut peaks beneath his tongue.

She arched her body as he slipped the bottom of her bikini down and his fingers slid between her thighs. There was no doubt those gently probing fingers would find her warm and wet with desire but...

She tensed suddenly because, although nothing else had changed, the music hadn't come...

'Caiti?'

Her lashes fluttered up.

'What are you thinking?' He withdrew his hand and put his arms around her.

'I...' She licked her lips. 'I don't know. Nothing. That is...someone might come looking for us.'

His gaze held hers intently and there was a frown at the back of his eyes. But after what seemed like an age, he kissed her gently on the lips and released her.

'Anything is possible with this mob,' he agreed and got up, holding his hand down to her. She wriggled back into her trousers and picked up her top.

'I think,' he said slowly as they stood side by side and she put on her bikini top, 'a swim is called for.'

'I think you're right,' she said huskily, and broke away from his side to run into the water. He followed immediately.

Caiti dunked herself completely and when she came up she undid her plait and soaked her hair to get the sand out of it. They came out together and he took her hand.

She opened her mouth to say she knew not what but he forestalled her, his gaze travelling down the lovely wet length of her before returning to her eyes. 'Don't.'

'What?' she whispered.

'I don't think words are going to be adequate at the moment.'

She took her hand back, picked up her sarong and took it to the water's edge, where she rinsed it out, squeezed it and patted her hair with it. Then she wound it around her and knotted it between her breasts. 'Perhaps not.'

'Except these—you're so beautiful.' He took her hand again and raised it to his lips. 'OK.' A glint of humour lit his eyes. 'Back to the fray.'

But the 'fray', as he'd put it, was a reconciliation in fact. Even Grace Handy, albeit stiffly, apologised to Caiti.

CHAPTER SEVEN

DINNER that evening was held in the main dining room.

A late booking had come through—a party of four, two couples in their late twenties who were more than happy to join up with the bridal party and turn the evening into a real party.

In fact it got so lively, they rolled back the rugs and danced after dinner.

But after doing her bit, Caiti yawned convincingly at about eleven o'clock and got Marion's blessing to go to bed. Instead of doing that and after ascertaining that Rob was still with the party, she walked down to the beach.

It was a mistake, she realised almost immediately. It brought back all the pain and turmoil of the day she'd left Rob and brought tears to her eyes.

She dashed at them and turned to go to her cabin but a shadow detached itself from the tree line—Rob.

She closed her eyes as he walked up to her then felt his fingers on her face. 'Rob…'

'Caiti, if I have to kidnap you, I'll do it. Right now, in fact.' He put his hand on her arm. 'You can walk or I'll carry you but I need to talk to you.'

She glanced at his grim expression and decided not to take the chance that he wouldn't be as good as his word. 'I'll walk.'

He took her to the reading room off the main lounge. It was beautifully furnished with deep, comfortable armchairs covered in cream velvet on a magenta carpet. Two walls were covered with built-in bookshelves and there was a lovely silky oak writing table with cabriole legs.

He pointed to a chair and told her he'd be back in a moment.

Fortunately, perhaps, Caiti was still feeling too shaken to take exception to his manner. She sat down and looked around.

They'd often shared a nightcap in here after all the guests had gone to bed. They'd often talked books but he'd also made love to her in this room once in the days before their wedding. He'd locked the door, kissed her deeply and such had been their need for each other they'd made love on the floor...

She closed her eyes and could feel the soft tickle of the carpet on her skin again, and she remembered, as their storm of passion had subsided, how they'd laughed together softly at the mad, impetuous whim that had overtaken them.

She came back to the present, and couldn't doubt that Rob had brought her here expressly to revive those memories.

He came back with two Irish coffees and closed the door.

She took hers and sipped it gratefully while he sat down opposite.

Presently he raised his head from the dark contemplation of his drink, and his gaze captured hers. 'I'm sorry, Caiti, you were right. It did seem—practical to ask you to marry me at the time, although it was never *only* that.'

She went still and her voice, when she spoke, sounded curiously far away. 'So you hadn't fallen in love with me?'

'Perhaps it would be more accurate to say—I had no intention of falling in love with anyone. But the way things happened—'

'You mean you found you'd seduced a virgin who'd fallen madly in love with you at the same time as you had to go home and face your brother's wife, who still lusted after you? I'm sorry to repeat myself or sound bitterly righteous, Rob, but that is the way things happened, isn't it?' she asked, and was immediately stunned at the intentional cruelty of it but couldn't find the words to retract any of it.

'Would you rather I'd said—*sorry, Caiti, something's come up, it's been nice to know you but you should just toddle off now*?'

She drew a shaky breath.

'Would that have hurt you any less?' he added.

She closed her eyes. Intentional or otherwise, the cruel reality of his shot hit home unerringly.

'No,' she whispered. 'But at least I wouldn't have had to come back to get a divorce from you.'

He put his coffee down on a side-table. 'Caiti, my sister-in-law is no longer in the equation either from the point of view of what she once meant to me—I got over that years ago—or fielding her advances. Leicester Downs is up and running smoothly again and doesn't need me, so there is no practical or *convenient* reason in the world why we should stay married now.'

She stood up and faced him squarely. 'That may be but what about the legacy she left you? Has that changed? You've just told me you didn't want to fall in love with anyone at the time—but will *you* ever change?'

'One thing hasn't changed,' he said drily. 'We still can't keep our hands off each other. Had you noticed that?'

She put her hands to her face as her cheeks warmed.

'So how do you account for it, Caiti?' He raised a derisive eyebrow.

'The other thing that interests me,' he went on when she couldn't answer, 'is the lack of detail about the man you plan to marry. Who is he, where is he and how serious is he, Caiti?'

She swallowed.

'Because he's not holding up much of a threat when I have you in my arms,' he added significantly and raked her from head to toe so that the light long dress she was wearing, cream with shadowy violet flowers, might just as well have been ripped from her body.

'He certainly didn't seem to come between us when you kissed me earlier in the day,' he continued, his eyes glinting with irony. 'Talking of serious, I would have said you were quite serious about that at the time. I know I was.'

She made a sound of supreme frustration in her throat. 'How like a man!'

'There could be a better way of putting it—how like a woman,' he said softly and got up to take her chin in his fingers. 'You may go to bed alone, Caiti Galloway, if you wish. But I know damn well where you'd rather be. So would I—talking of which,' he looked around, 'do you remember a certain night in here—? Ah, I see you do,' he said as she pulled away hastily.

'That's…' She couldn't go on.

He studied her meditatively. 'Hitting below the belt again?' He shrugged. 'All the same, it doesn't seem to have gone away, so don't you think that's a fairly crucial state of affairs between us?'

She put her hands to her temples. 'Rob, you—'

'Yes, all right,' he broke in, 'I may have some baggage that I don't find easy to talk about. And it's quite conceivable I've been rather cynical about love, marriage, happy families and the like at times, but after eighteen *months* for us still to feel like this, surely that's a fair test of what we mean to each other in *real* terms?'

'Real terms?' she whispered.

'I want you as much as I ever did, Caiti. Not only in my bed but also in my life. And whenever you let your guard down, it's the same for you—isn't it?' He eyed her critically.

She pressed her hands together but could find no words to deny it.

'Let me put something else to you in real terms,' he added softly. 'There's an old saying about a woman scorned—and it seems to me that's how you felt, rightly or wrongly. So, is it revenge?'

'Revenge,' she repeated huskily. 'What do you mean?'

'Wanting to divorce me for another man?'

Her mouth fell open. But what she would have done if the phone on the desk hadn't rung discreetly and he was called away, she was not to know.

Especially when he smiled tigerishly at her and murmured, 'Saved by the bell, no doubt.'

Once she got to her cabin, she found herself trembling almost uncontrollably.

Because the truth was, she was no match for Rob Leicester in tiger mode. And the truth was, the attraction between them hadn't changed—he was right about that. It was as strong as ever. But was she right in thinking other things hadn't changed either?

His cynicism, for example? The fact that he still couldn't see his inability to say, or believe, that he loved her was because, for whatever reason, he simply didn't believe in it?

Or maybe love's just not there, she reasoned with tears falling down her cheeks, and never will be. But if that's so, is there more in his past to account for it or does it mean he has a yardstick to measure what he feels for me against what he felt for some other woman? What he felt for his sister-in-law, perhaps, even if he's convinced he's over it?

She rubbed her face and her confused thoughts moved on the mayhem she'd created by letting him go on thinking she wanted to remarry. At the time the fleeting thought had seemed like a form of self-protection. Then she'd rejected it only to be goaded into going along with it, never to dream he would turn it into such an effective weapon to use against her…

The other aspect, she reflected, was, as well as using it as a weapon against her, how else was it distorting things between them? For instance, she was desperately trying to deal with the essence of Rob Leicester. Was he a man who loved her but couldn't say it; or a man who would never allow himself to take that ultimate step in a relationship with a woman?

Whereas he was now accusing her of planning to avenge herself against him by marrying someone else—surely it had to add a distortion to his feelings?

She sat down on her bed and hugged herself, taking deep breaths to still the trembling, and posed an even more difficult question to herself—could Rob be forgiven for doing the honourable thing by marrying her rather than telling her to 'toddle off'?

She must have been, after all, on his mind ever since she left him. Why else would he have named a new camp after her, or still want her as much as he did. Was she being a fool to spurn everything he had to offer her, including their almost explosive desire for each other, because it came under the name of realism for him?

No answer presented itself as she listened to the staccato chirping of a gecko, and her sleep, when it came, was patchy and dream-laden.

The next morning things took another turn.

You would have had to be blind not to realise that Marion and Derek had had an almighty row.

Caiti watched her cousin's set, pale face over breakfast and took the first opportunity to draw her aside afterwards.

'What?' she asked as they strolled down one of the wooden boardwalks through the rainforest. 'What's happened? Why are you looking like this?'

'I'm not going to marry Derek,' Marion said tautly. 'And if you think I care, you're mistaken.'

'Marion, yes, I do think you care!' Caiti protested. 'How did it happen? Surely it can be fixed?'

Marion stopped walking and faced Caiti squarely. 'No, it cannot! Nothing I do seems to be right these days and that's not all. I don't even think he wants children!'

She set off again at a fast pace so that Caiti had to jog a bit to keep up.

'Look,' Caiti said as a bench came into sight, 'let's sit down and take things one at a time. What don't you do right?'

But Marion continued walking although she said over her shoulder, 'He doesn't think it's appropriate for me to be wearing my honeymoon clothes before the wedding. He's afraid I may have splurged too much money on them, anyway. He even thinks we may be spending too much on the honeymoon itself.'

'Oh.'

'Then he had to the gall to tell me he didn't think my behaviour last night was appropriate for a soon-to-be married woman.'

'What?'

'I danced with two other men last night. It was fun—everyone was dancing with everyone else, except Derek.'

'OK. OK!' Caiti took Marion by the shoulders and propelled her back to the bench. 'What makes you think he doesn't want children?'

'Last night, before all this blew up, I said to him that this time next year, it would be nice to come back to Camp Ondine for a combined wedding-anniversary-christening party, and if you and Rob were together you'd make perfect godparents.'

Caiti's eyes widened and she was speechless.

'Granted,' Marion went on, 'I'd had a few glasses of wine, I was happy and…and, well, you know what it's like when these things just spring into your head and you say them?'

Caiti nodded after a moment.

'That's when he said—*let's not start thinking about kids yet, Marion. We've got years before we need to go down that road.*'

'Marion—'

But Marion turned to her intensely. 'Caiti, to be honest I would have been happy to be married long before this. Now I know that Derek has been having his cake and eating it! Perhaps I even made it too easy for him, I don't know, but I now know this— all the real emotion between us has been on my side. All the joy and happiness about getting married has been mine. Derek—is not seeing it that way.'

'But…' Caiti stopped abruptly as she remembered Rob's reading of the situation and how it coincided with this…

'Furthermore,' Marion said, 'if he thinks I don't know what all this nit-picking is about, he's mistaken. It's designed to make me so mad *I* will be the one to call it off thereby leaving him to look like the injured party.'

'Honey,' Caiti said on a breath, 'what will you do?'

Marion blew her nose and wiped her eyes. 'I am going to call it off.'

'But…do you still love him?'

'I don't know. I don't know if I'm so used to thinking I love him it's become habit. I don't know if the worst thought isn't—what a waste of my life it's been. There's not much I know at the moment but I'm sick of doing everything to Derek's agenda. I will *not* be told when to start a family!'

'Sweetheart,' Caiti said softly and put her arm around Marion's shoulders, 'I'm so sorry. I don't know what to say. I guess only you can make this decision.'

Marion sniffed and closed her eyes. 'What about you and Rob?'

'Uh…nothing resolved there yet.' She paused and frowned.

Marion put her hanky away. 'But you're talking?'

Caiti flinched inwardly as she nodded then changed the subject. 'Have you told Derek that you're going to call it off?'

'Not yet. I'll wait until we get home. The last thing I want is an audience of his mother and sister. Listen, why don't you stay here another night or two?'

'Oh, no! I mean, I haven't been asked, and anyway you—'

Marion gripped her hand at the same time as she said, 'I love you and I thank you but I don't need you to hold my hand, Caiti. I know what I'm doing. And after I've done it, I'm going to hop on a plane and go to Brisbane for a day or two.'

This was said with so much decision, Caiti realised

that this was one of those few occasions when her cousin was in formidable mode.

'Well—'

'Look,' Marion stood up, 'at least Rob didn't string you along for four years then find he couldn't commit!'

'Maybe Derek didn't realise...' Caiti broke off helplessly.

'It doesn't matter.'

'At least, before you break it off, just tell it to him as you've told it to me,' Caiti pleaded. 'He may surprise you.'

Marion raised her eyebrows in an indication that nothing would ever surprise her again, then they heard footsteps. 'Uh-oh, here comes someone!'

Fortunately it was one of the guest couples out for a morning stroll. They exchanged pleasantries then Marion and Caiti walked back to the lounge in silence.

Until Caiti said, 'Will you be able to pretend nothing is wrong until you get home?'

'Oh, Derek knows things are wrong. We'll just have to rely on Ritchie to keep us going. Now, you don't really want to be part of that kind of awkwardness, do you, Caiti?'

Before Caiti got a chance to answer, they bumped into Rob, crossing the lounge.

'Just the person I was looking for,' Marion said. 'Rob, could you put Caiti up for a couple more nights?'

'Marion! Rob, I…um…' Caiti ran out of words.

But although Rob looked startled then narrowly at Caiti, he said immediately, 'With pleasure, if you don't need her in Cairns.'

'No. I'm fine,' Marion assured him. 'She's done such a sterling job up to now,' she added conspiratorially, 'I reckon she deserves a little break away from us.'

'Marion,' Caiti said, but Marion was off in the direction of her cabin.

'I need to pack! See you soon.'

Caiti released a very deep breath.

'I hesitate to ask,' Rob said.

'You were right. Well, at least Marion is convinced that Derek is a reluctant starter for this wedding and she's going to call it off. I can't believe it!'

'Better now than later.'

'You could hardly be much later than a week or so before the wedding but, yes, I know what you mean. I'm exhausted,' she said and realised she meant it. 'But don't say anything, it's not common knowledge yet. Look, about staying—'

'Just try *not* staying, Caiti.'

'Rob, this caveman mode doesn't become you!' She stared up at him with extreme frustration.

He folded his arms and drawled, 'Desperate times call for desperate measures and we do have some unfinished business between us. If you would excuse me for a moment, I'm needed in the office—but don't even think of doing a runner, Caiti.'

*   *   *

'What's your name?'

Caiti was sitting on a rock beside the beach, lost in contemplation of the mysteries of life, and nuptials in particular, when this question was put to her. It was mid-afternoon and Marion's party had left in an obviously subdued manner a few hours ago.

She turned to see a little girl of about six in a frilly bikini. She had fair curly hair, blue eyes and appeared to be alone.

'Oh! Hello. My name is Caiti. What's yours?'

The child drew nearer. 'Miranda. Do you live here?'

'No. I'm just a guest—how about you?'

'Well, I think I am too. Mummy said she couldn't stand the station any longer so we were coming here whether anyone liked it or not,' Miranda revealed. 'Do you believe in fairies?'

Caiti opened her mouth, closed it and said quite seriously, 'Yes, I do.'

'A lot of people don't,' Miranda said, almost accusingly.

Caiti frowned. 'A lot of people think it's "grown up" not to believe in fairies. What they don't realise is that the fairies know this, so they leave them alone. For example, the tooth fairy doesn't come once you don't believe in her any more.'

'Well, I thought I did but she still didn't come. See?' Miranda opened her mouth very wide to reveal a lost front tooth. 'That happened two days ago but no one has come to collect my tooth!'

'Ah. Do you know what I think has happened? The fairies must be *very* busy. I would say that if you put your tooth out tonight, they will almost certainly come and collect it.'

'The tooth!' another voice said distractedly and a fair, harassed-looking woman erupted onto the beach from the path. 'Damn—uh, oh—hi!' she said to Caiti before rounding on the child. 'Miranda, how many times have I told you you're not allowed to wander off on your own?'

'I'm not on my own, Mummy,' Miranda pointed out. 'I'm with this lady. Her name is Caiti.'

Caiti held out her hand. 'Caiti Galloway. How do you do?'

'Do you mean…are you…are *you* Caiti Galloway?'

'Yes, I am!' Caiti responded with a faint smile. 'What have I done now?'

'No, nothing! I mean…oh, heavens!' The other woman looked skywards. 'This has not been my best day, I do apologise. I'm Alexandra Leicester, Lex for short. I'm Rob's stepmother… Well, I've left his father, but anyway. Have you…have you come back to Rob?'

'Don't know about that,' Miranda slid her hand into Caiti's, 'but she does believe in fairies.'

I also believe I'm *away* with the fairies, Caiti thought in absolute confusion.

CHAPTER EIGHT

'THINGS are—getting out of hand,' Caiti said to her husband.

It was the first opportunity she'd had to be alone with Rob during what had started out as a difficult, bewildering day then become a very busy one, for Rob, at least. A tour party of ten arriving on top of his stepmother and half-sister turning up out of the blue being the cause.

But it was the quiet hour before dinner when everyone was showering and dressing, and he'd conducted her to a secluded corner of the deck screened by a creeper from the rest of it and overlooking the river mouth. He handed her a cocktail.

'You're not wrong,' he agreed with a grimace and stretched his long legs out. 'Do you think there's something in the air? Or the water?'

'I'm beginning to wonder,' Caiti said faintly.

'Mind you, Lex has walked out on my father a couple of times before but she's always gone back.'

'Why has she walked out?'

He plucked the cherry on a stick out of his drink and ate it. 'The usual trouble women have with their Leicester men. Dad's domineering, he's work-fixated, he doesn't understand the pressures living on

133

a cattle station in the middle of nowhere put on her. And thanks to him, she forgot to play the tooth fairy to Miranda.'

He punched some tiny holes in the wooden arm of his chair with the tooth pick then raised his eyes to her. 'Ever longed for a desert island?'

Caiti looked heavenwards. 'What a pleasant prospect!' She sobered rapidly. 'But—why would she come to stay with you?'

He tossed the tooth pick over the railing. 'What am I? Some kind of monster?'

'I didn't say that,' Caiti objected. 'But she must have, if nothing else, displaced your mother—'

'She didn't. That was well and truly over before Lex came into our lives.'

Caiti paused, then, 'What about having a half-sister of six?'

He grinned suddenly. 'It makes me feel a bit ancient at times but for all that I like Lex.'

'Thank heavens someone does!' Lex swept round the creeper carrying her own cocktail and plonked herself down in a chair.

'Lex,' Rob stood up, 'talking of your daughter and her propensity for wandering off, where is she?'

'One of the housemaids is looking after her. I warned her not to let Miranda out of her sight.'

'OK. Will you both excuse me for a while, and I'll join you for dinner?'

'Yes, you toddle off, Rob, and I'll get to know Caiti better,' Lex said.

The look Rob cast Caiti before he walked off was one of pure devilry.

'You know,' Lex confided, 'there are times when I wish I'd married Rob rather than his father, Frank.'

Caiti stared at her wide-eyed. 'Did you…have the opportunity?'

Lex shook her head. 'Only joking! So tell me about yourself, Caiti.'

Caiti studied Frank Leicester's wife while she debated how to handle this. Lex looked to be in her late thirties, she was tall and slender, and as fair as her daughter with the same blue eyes. She was also attractive although in a rather no-nonsense way—you got the feeling from her direct blue gaze that Lex Leicester spoke her mind.

Then she said quietly, 'Rob wants us to stay married but I have the gravest reservations.'

Lex observed her sharply then sipped her drink. 'Why?'

Caiti sighed suddenly. 'You probably know all that even better than I do.'

'You mean Steve and particularly Stella?'

'Is that her name? Steve's wife?'

'Yes. All that is over and done with,' Lex said authoritatively.

Caiti shrugged and Lex nodded in sudden agreement.

'You're right if you mean Rob should be convincing you not me. But,' Lex sipped her drink, 'nine out of ten women would say you're mad.'

'Would *you*, though?'

Lex sighed. 'They're all difficult. I think it runs in the family.'

Caiti frowned faintly. 'Is—Frank the same?'

'He can be.' Lex studied her hands. 'You see, when you've wrested an untamed country from a wilderness, when you've battled drought, flood, sometimes shocking heat, not to mention the vagaries of cattle prices, diseases and so on, it toughens you almost too much. On top of that, though, for Rob there was all the nonsense about whose son he was and the marriage break-up. It was bound to leave a mark on him.'

Caiti paused in the act of taking up her glass with her eyes wide and shocked, but Lex appeared not to notice as she continued.

'Of the three of them, though, I sometimes think Rob is the sanest, well, the most far-seeing, anyway. It was his idea to diversify and I would say Leicester Camps are proving to be a gold-mine. He's also the only one, probably because he left Leicester Downs with his mother for a time, who can take it or leave it.' She looked around. 'So you wouldn't be wedded to a cattle station, which, believe me, has to be a plus. Ah, here he comes.'

Caiti turned to see Rob walking across the deck towards him with Miranda in tow, who was talking very earnestly to him. He replied with equal gravity but whatever he said caused Miranda to trill with laughter and look up at him delightedly.

A strange sensation came over Caiti, as if she was viewing a different man but at the same time piecing together a jigsaw puzzle as Marion's words yesterday came back to her. How much more baggage was there in his background, she wondered, to contribute towards a man who, perhaps, had walled himself off from ever allowing himself to get too close to anyone?

Three days later Caiti was still at Camp Ondine. So were Lex and Miranda, although overtures from Frank Leicester had been received and were being mulled over.

And news had come from Marion that the wedding had not, as yet, been called off but she still wasn't sure it would go ahead.

'There are only five days left!' Caiti commented when she relayed the news to Rob.

'Cutting it a bit fine,' he agreed. 'Derek must have got a bit of a shock, faced with the reality of losing her, and is pulling out all the stops.'

Caiti opened her mouth then closed it as his last sentence struck a curious chord with her. If Derek was using all his power to persuade Marion he loved her enough to marry her, Rob was not noticeably trying to persuade her, Caiti Galloway, of anything.

In fact, he'd put her to work.

Well, she amended her thoughts, when a staffing crisis had blown up—the remoteness of the camp made it particularly vulnerable to staff crises—he'd asked her if she could fill in for him on a guided ramble through the rainforest. She'd agreed happily.

A distinct flash of humour had lit his eyes before he'd thanked her gravely.

'What's that supposed to mean?'

'Just one thing,' he said. 'What about the wild-life?'

'Yuk!' Miranda, who was with them at the time, said with feeling. 'I found a frog in my wellington once. I put my foot on it and I nearly got a heart attack.'

'Had a heart attack,' Lex corrected, 'but you're far too young to be having one of those, darling.'

'Why?'

Caiti smiled inwardly. Miranda was an exceed-ingly curious child. Simple explanations rarely sat-isfied her and her favourite question after *why?* was *and then what?* until you were tempted to tear out your hair. But Rob suggesting they go for a swim saved them the inevitable round of explanations.

Not only did she slip into doing the twice-daily rainforest ramble, but she also got called in to help out at the reception desk.

Due to exercising the utmost concentration, partic-ularly with the switchboard, she had no disasters and her rambles were highly successful.

Something Rob commented on. 'I see you haven't lost your touch. With people,' he added.

'Neither have I overbooked you, double-booked

you, underbooked you nor caused any disasters for the kitchen,' she replied tartly.

'You're a treasure, Miss Galloway.' Then his eyes changed. 'Or should I say, Mrs Leicester?'

Caiti held her breath but he said no more. As for his suggestion they continue their marriage, that appeared to be off the, at least, conversation agenda entirely at the moment.

Then it struck her that Rob Leicester might be pursuing his agenda with a lot of subtlety, if not to say downright devious intent. Because in so many ways she was reminded of how they'd worked together eighteen months ago. Strictly on a business basis but with the growing torture of sublimating their desire for each other at the same time.

It was happening to her again, she had to acknowledge now, although, at the same time, she admitted it probably always would in his company. But working with him seemed to add an extra *frisson*, she thought as she closed herself into her cabin that night.

It had been a long day. Camp Ondine was full, but not only that, it seemed to be full of especially demanding guests. She also happened to know from the amount of time he spent on the phone that Rob was having trouble with the last stages of Camp Caiti; that and the fact that he seemed to be unusually preoccupied.

She went to the window and breathed in the night air, conscious that she was now experiencing a different kind of turmoil. Not only was there the picture she had in her mind of a boy growing up with the burden of his father's doubts about whose son he was, but she was also suddenly seeing a more complete Rob Leicester.

Thanks to Lex and Miranda; when he was in their company he was funny, that moody look never touched his eyes and he was really good with his half-sister, who adored him.

In fact she was liking the more complete man a lot, but... To the point where she could forgive him? To the point of believing in him? Or, perhaps more importantly, could they ever get to a stage where he could confide completely in her?

It was a question she was not destined to answer at the time because as she leant out of the window something jumped onto the window sill beside her.

She slammed the window shut and tore out of the cabin onto the veranda, to bump into Rob.

'Whoa!' He fielded her. 'Steady on, Caiti. What's happened?'

She told him and shuddered. 'A frog... I thought I'd got over it! Yuk! Miranda's right. Do you think *I'm* too young to get a heart attack?'

'Yes. But your heart is beating very fast!'

'You can feel it?'

He spread his hands across her back and pulled her into him. 'Yes.'

Nothing on earth could have prevented her from nestling her head against his shoulder as her breathing settled and her heart rate slowed. 'I feel very silly,' she said barely audibly.

'On the contrary,' his hands moved, 'you feel gorgeous.'

'Rob?' She took a breath and looked up into his eyes.

He looked down at her for a long moment, his gaze hooded but intent. 'I don't know about you, Caiti, but this is going to be one of those times when I can't help myself, so—you have a choice but not for long.'

She shuddered again but this time for a very different reason. This time she was achingly conscious of the heat and strength of his body, his undoubted desire for her, and the way her body was answering for her.

'I...' Her lavender eyes were suddenly wet and anguished. 'I don't—'

'Caiti,' his voice was suddenly rough, 'walk away now if you want to.' He opened his arms. 'Because if you don't it's going to happen.'

She stared up at him and saw the tension around his mouth and the strain in his eyes.

'Can I ask one question?' she said huskily. 'Where has all this been since the last few days?'

'Been?' He smiled almost ferociously. 'Buried under work and a lot of willpower. How did you do it?'

'The...the same, I guess,' she faltered then

shrugged and was completely honest. 'Working with you made it worse, harder.'

'So?'

'Why can't you tell me why you are the way you are, Rob?'

'Caiti, what has saying...?' He broke off and set his teeth. 'OK, I'm cynical, disillusioned, my parents' relationship was something of a nightmare, my brother's wife turned into one—what more do you want to know?'

'Did you really love her? Stella.'

He heaved a sigh. 'At the time, I thought so. She was—' he shrugged '—bewitching, and then to discover she was a two-timing witch on top of everything...' He stopped briefly and his teeth shut hard. 'But it's over, Caiti.'

On top of not knowing if you're your father's son, she thought sadly, it could have been devastating, but you still can't tell me about that...

'So what is it between us?' she queried. 'As *you* see it?'

'I see it as a definite,' he paused and his gaze roamed over her, 'desire to bring back the music.'

Her lips parted. 'You knew?' she whispered.

'I guessed. There are so many things I could never forget about you.'

She half turned away. 'Too much for my own good. Rob,' her voice was clogged with emotion, 'there's so much I still don't understand and I could never be sure that this isn't pity, or *honour*, or both.'

'So what *do* you have in mind for us?' he asked harshly.

The question took her by surprise. 'What do you mean?'

'Caiti, we can't go on like this,' he said deliberately. 'What do you suggest we do about it?'

She could only stare at him.

'Are you suggesting we ignore it and once this bloody wedding is either on or off, we go our separate ways? You—to a man you forget all about every time I kiss you?'

Her lips parted then she swallowed and said, 'Yes...'

'Then your vengeance will be complete?' he drawled. 'Isn't that a high price to pay?'

She lost her temper suddenly. 'I'm sure you'll get over this little setback, Rob. I'm sure, and so is your stepmother, that there are many women out there who would be more than happy to console you, so—'

'And you, Caiti?' The expression in his eyes was hard and insolent. 'Who will you choose to console you?'

'I don't know.' She licked the salt of her tears off her lip. 'I don't know.'

'What about—?'

'There is no one. You just assumed I wanted a divorce to remarry, I didn't ever say it.'

Over the next moments, as he digested this, if anything his expression hardened. 'But you've let me go on thinking it?'

She opened her hands, palms out. 'I thought it might help to make you see...sense.'

'Sense?' he repeated softly but almost murderously. And this time he was the one to turn on his heel and stride swiftly down the steps into the night.

Clint Walker had worked for Rob Leicester through the setting up of Camp Ondine and two others, and he'd run Ondine when Rob had gone home to help his father run Leicester Downs.

He had great respect for his boss, for the way he worked as hard as anyone and the vision behind the project, despite the fact that he could be tough and autocratic at times.

Therefore, he was in two minds when Caiti Galloway approached him that evening with an urgent request for help to leave Camp Ondine.

He liked Caiti. He had, after all, given her away and been best man at her wedding to Rob eighteen months ago. What had gone wrong a mere two days later was still a mystery to him but it had saddened him. He'd thought they were well-suited and he'd crossed his fingers that her reappearance at Camp Ondine would lead to them getting back together.

But the Caiti Galloway who cornered him in the bowels of the laundry, where he was battling with a recalcitrant industrial washer, was obviously not a happy girl.

She had dark circles under her eyes and she was so tense you wouldn't be surprised to see her snap.

'Caiti,' he looked at his watch, 'I can't do it to-night. Not only have I got to get this washer fixed but I also have all sorts of other things to do. Anyway, you cleared this with the boss?'

'Clint, I'm running away from "the boss"!'

'Oh, Caiti—not again!' His expression creased into genuine concern. 'Listen, I don't know what's with you two but he isn't that bad.'

'Clint...' Caiti breathed heavily, then said exasperatedly, 'If only this wasn't a wilderness camp!'

'Wouldn't be as popular otherwise,' he pointed out. 'Look, why don't you sleep on it? It's a helluva long drive to Port Douglas and, to be honest, my job mightn't be worth a row of beans if I do help you get away at this time of night. Any time, for that matter.'

Caiti counted to three beneath her breath then looked guilty and contrite. 'Look, I'm sorry, I shouldn't have asked you. I guess I wasn't thinking too straight.'

Clint patted her on her shoulder. 'Go to bed, Caiti. Things always look worse at night.'

'I...I...will.'

Three hours later Clint Walker knocked at his boss's cabin door with deep trepidation.

A light went on in the darkened cabin and a few moments later a tousled Rob Leicester, wearing only shorts, appeared.

He regarded his off-sider with disfavour. 'OK. Hit

me with it. It's been a hell of a day—why should it
be about to end?'

Clint grimaced. 'Nothing broken down, Rob, but
one of the vehicles has disappeared.'

Rob's eyebrows shot skywards. 'Come again?'

'Your four-wheel drive, to be precise.'

'What?'

'Uh-huh,' Clint agreed.

'So one of the guests is a raving kleptomaniac?
They could—anything could happen on these roads
in the dark!'

'Not precisely one of the guests,' Clint said awkwardly.

Rob frowned then ruffled his already ruffled hair
devoutly. 'Who—to be precise?' he shot back.

Clint looked a picture of discomfort as he started
to relate his earlier encounter with Caiti.

Rob heard him out with growing disbelief. At the
end of it, he said, 'You're wrong, Clint. She's fast
asleep next door.'

'Have you actually seen her?'

'Hard to do through a no doubt locked door,' Rob
replied cynically, 'but I'll prove it to you.' He
stepped out of his doorway and rapped on the next
door. 'Caiti, open up!' he called. 'Clint thinks you've
gone AWOL.'

There was no response so Rob knocked again then
tried the handle. It opened. He put his hand inside
and groped for the light switch. When he found it,
the overhead light revealed a painfully neat and ob-

viously empty room. The bed was made, the dresser was bare, there were no clothes, no bags, nothing other than the furniture it came with.

'She couldn't have gone far,' Clint ventured. 'I'm pretty sure your car was there half an hour ago when I passed through the garage.'

Rob swore fluently.

Clint said tentatively, 'Could I give you a piece of advice?'

'Why *not*?'

An expression of regret that he had ever opened his mouth crossed Clint's face. 'It doesn't matter,' he said hastily.

'Clint, speak now or for ever hold your peace,' Rob ordered.

'Well, she was really upset. Maybe, just maybe you need to change your—uh—approach.'

'What the bloody hell do you think I've been trying to do?' Rob demanded, and stalked back into his room, where he started to pull clothes on at random. Ten minutes later he was driving a second four-wheel-drive vehicle down the rough track that led to the Cape Tribulation road.

Caiti had driven over this road many a time but always with someone else doing the driving. Not only that, but she'd also never driven a four-wheel drive before and suspected she was not using the correct gears for maximum handling of the terrain.

So, with intense concentration, she inched the vehicle over bumps, potholes, craters, rocks and the like. The forest towered above the road on either side and every now and then her headlights picked up pairs of red eyes—kangaroos and wallabies. She shivered to think of everything else it harboured.

On the other hand, she was pretty confident no one would miss her until the next morning. The garage at the camp was next to the generator room, as far removed from the guest quarters as possible, so the hum of the generator wouldn't disturb anyone. It had masked, though, she felt, starting the car engine with the keys left conveniently in it.

She'd also been reasonably confident that Clint had finally stopped pottering around and gone to bed. Rob, she knew, had done the same.

Therefore, it came as unpleasant shock when she saw headlights approaching in her rear-view mirror, and coming a lot faster than she was daring to drive.

'Damn, damn, damn!' she muttered, then prayed, since she hadn't reached the required turn-off yet, that it could only be Clint.

Of course it wasn't. The second vehicle passed her where it didn't seem possible to then slewed across the road, blocking her passage so she had to jam on her brakes, and Rob jumped out.

She was still shaking from reaction when he pulled open her door.

'Running away again, Caiti?'

She gripped the steering wheel and bit into her lip until she almost drew blood—and snapped. '*Yes!*

Why shouldn't I? I'm not your prisoner... I hate you...' tears poured down her cheeks and she wiped her nose on the back of her hand '...I hate being married to you and you've just scared six months out of me.'

He reached in and turned the motor off. 'None of that justifies doing this. Ever driven one of these before?'

'No! But I would have got there somehow!'

'Or killed yourself in the process,' he said curtly.

Caiti folded her arms over the steering wheel, laid her forehead on them and wept.

Rob regarded her shaking shoulders silently. Then he sighed and moved away but she didn't even notice as he repositioned the second vehicle off the road, locked it and came back to her.

Nor did she have the energy or fighting spirit left when he carefully lifted her out of the driver's seat and carried her round to the passenger side. Then he fiddled with a cabinet built into the back of the front seats, extracted something from it and got into the driver's seat, where he clicked on the interior light.

'Caiti,' he said quietly, and stroked her hair, 'have some of this.'

She blinked away the tears long enough to see he was holding out a hip-flask to her.

'What?'

'Brandy, that's all. It'll help.'

He put the flask to her lips and she swallowed

obediently. Then she had a second sip, and the worst of her tear storm started to subside.

He put the flask on the dashboard, took her in his arms and said barely audibly into her hair, 'What are we going to do?'

'I d-don't k-know,' she stammered.

'Do you really hate me?'

She closed her eyes.

'Caiti?'

'No, Rob,' she didn't open her eyes, 'but I'm really afraid to...love you again.'

'Perhaps,' he paused and kissed her damp eyelids softly, 'that's my fault. Can I at least start again?'

She took a ragged breath and her lashes fluttered up.

The little golden flecks in his eyes were most noticeable and his gaze was deep and compelling.

'How?' she whispered.

'I think,' he hesitated, 'I need to go right back to the beginning, my beginning. Not right now, though. You need a good night's sleep first. But will you let me do that?'

She swallowed a couple of times, then nodded.

He was as good as his word.

He drove her back to camp and virtually put her to bed. She fell asleep almost before her head touched the pillow but he stayed for a while to make sure she didn't waken. Then he left a candle burning and went to grab the few hours left to him of the night.

*   *   *

Caiti woke up the next morning feeling as bruised and battered as if all her emotional encounters of the previous day had been physical ones.

In fact, she didn't have the energy to get out of bed and was sitting up against the pillows when Rob knocked briefly and came in with a breakfast tray. Miranda was with him.

'Caiti,' she said enthusiastically and climbed onto the bed to hug her, 'you were right! I've been meaning to tell you but I kept forgetting.'

'I was?' Caiti hugged her back.

'Yes.' Miranda sat back on her heels and pulled a shiny two-dollar coin out of her pocket. 'The tooth fairy came! They mustn't have been so busy.'

'Goodness me,' Caiti enthused. 'They certainly paid well too!'

'Mummy said that's because it's my first tooth and they were late. Prob'ly, I shouldn't expect so much money the next time.'

'Talk about conscience money—twenty cents used to be the going rate,' Rob put in ruefully and placed the tray on the bedside table. He straightened and looked down at her enquiringly. 'How are you?'

'Fine,' she assured him hastily and gathered her hair back. 'Probably better than I look.'

'You look...' He stopped himself. 'Uh—would you be free for a private lunch later?'

'How—could it be private?'

'I've decided to go fishing. Just you and me and

a packed lunch. We'll take the small launch up the river.'

'Mummy and I can't come because Daddy is coming to see us,' Miranda confided.

Caiti's eyes widened and she looked swiftly at Rob.

He nodded then hesitated. 'The other news is not so good, however. Marion rang earlier. It's off.'

Caiti sat up urgently with her hand to her throat. 'How is she?'

'Winging her way to Brisbane as we speak. May I—tell you all about it when we have lunch?'

She sank back. 'OK...'

'In the meantime, relax,' he recommended and put the tray on her knees. 'Meet me at the jetty at twelve?'

Their gazes caught again, and held for a long moment.

'Yes...'

He left, taking Miranda with him.

Caiti looked down at the breakfast tray. There was an exquisite creamy hibiscus bloom on it with its stem bound in a yellow ribbon. She sniffed but absolutely refused to give way to tears.

CHAPTER NINE

THE small launch may have been smaller than the one that took cruises to the Hope Isles but it had lots of comfort. A compact galley and head, plenty of space on the back deck beneath an awning and a vee berth up front so you could overnight.

At ten past twelve, Caiti waved goodbye to Lex and Miranda and released the line tying the launch to the jetty. Rob nosed it into the centre of the river and gunned the motor.

She watched the twin curves of white wake behind them and held on to her hat. The river was as smooth as glass and reflecting the sky as the ripples from the wake spread out. It was hot and cloudless, a perfect day.

Frank Leicester had not arrived as yet and they'd left Lex looking tense while Miranda, blissfully unaware, was full of excited anticipation.

'Perhaps we should have brought Miranda with us,' she called suddenly to Rob, over the noise of the powerful outboard.

He looked over his shoulder ruefully. 'I appreciate your desire to fix all things marital but that's going above and beyond the call of duty.'

Caiti grimaced. 'I just feel for Lex.'

'One of the room maids is on hand to help out.'

'Oh. How far upstream are we going?' She moved up to stand beside him. 'And how did you manage to get the time off?'

'I'll let you into a little secret. Clint is suddenly full of suggestions. I was wondering aloud how I could snatch a few hours without being interrupted. He said—it's simple, do the proverbial ''gone fishing'' bit. He added that he would hold the fort.'

'He's rather a sweetie, isn't he?'

Rob nodded. 'As for how far upstream, I have a special spot I don't take anyone to and the fish abound.'

'Sounds good to me.'

He grinned down at her. 'The crocs also abound so we won't be able to swim.'

Half an hour later they were anchored in a bend of the river. It was a magical spot. Palm trees lined the bank, and in a little bay just upstream a riot of pink water lilies covered the surface. The only sounds were bird calls and the plop of an occasional fish rising to the surface.

They both had fishing lines in the water and Rob had just handed her a glass of chilled white wine and opened a beer for himself. The sun, the peace and perhaps an overexposure to too much emotion had Caiti feeling almost comatose.

Then she felt a tug on her line and her—fortunately plastic—tumbler went flying as she jumped up excitedly. 'What do I do now?'

'Just wind in slowly.' Rob put his beer down and reached for the landing net. 'Keep the weight on the tip of the rod and if you feel he's getting away from you, give him a bit more line. Not too much otherwise he'll head straight for those rocks on the bank. How big does he feel?'

Caiti started to puff as she wound the line in. 'Like a whale! I...I can't hold him.'

'Yes, you can. Just do as I say—a bit of slack now,' he instructed.

She gasped as the line took off. 'Wow! What is it?'

'Don't know. OK, wind again—steady on!'

So she wound with her wrists and hands aching under the pressure and the end of the rod, the tip of which was bent right over, digging into her tummy. Then in a sudden explosion the fish leapt out of the water and dived back in again, and she nearly fell over.

Rob moved round behind her to steady her with his hands on her hips. 'Keep winding, I'll keep you on your feet.'

'Is it a barramundi?' she panted, now scarlet in the face.

'Nope.'

'Oh!' She was obviously disappointed.

He laughed softly into her hair. 'If you believe some people, it's even better—a threadfin salmon, I reckon. Marvellous eating. OK, OK,' he said rapidly, 'we're getting close now. Keep winding and don't let him go under the boat—he'll snap the line on the prop.'

Caiti wound, although her heart felt like bursting until she could see the silver body of the fish just below the surface of the water.

'You're on your own for a moment.' Rob moved away from her and as quick as lightning, plunged the net into the water and brought up the fish.

Caiti sat down on her bottom on the deck as the pressure was released, and Rob swore.

'What—? Ouch! What's wrong?' she gabbled.

'Just the best damn salmon I've ever seen!' He laughed down at her, looking so alive and breathtakingly masculine that she breathed erratically.

Then he picked the fish up by its gills and held it aloft. 'Take a bow, Mrs Leicester, this is some catch! Are you all right?' he added belatedly.

Caiti struggled to her feet. 'Apart from some bruising of the derrière, which obviously escaped your notice,' she said severely, then broke out laughing. 'Why do men forget everything when there's a fish on a line?'

He put the fish down in a tank of water, took her into his arms and began to massage her bottom with one hand.

'There,' he said softly. 'Any better?'

'Mmm…' She nodded.

A glint of pure devilry lurked in his eyes. 'Would you like me to have a look?'

'Do you think that's wise?'

'Depends.' He paused and scanned her still flushed cheeks. 'On whether you want to talk first or—not.'

Caiti tumbled down from the euphoria of the fish; and, if she was honest, the euphoria of being in his arms.

She moistened her lips and was about to speak when it suddenly slammed into her consciousness that she loved Rob Leicester whether she liked it or not, whether it scared her silly or not, whether he could ever love her the same way.

And there was absolutely nothing she'd rather be doing than to be out on a boat, fishing with him like this. In fact, she'd rather be anywhere in the world with him than alone. Not only that, but her body was also humming with desire, the blood was singing through her veins, her legs felt unsteady and overall she felt like a neglected garden with the sap rising and springing to life at the prospect of his lovemaking.

'Rob,' she trembled down the length of her, 'I guess I've arrived at a—what-will-be-will-be stage.' She swallowed. 'I don't want any promises or declarations because right now all I want is you. Could you—would you give me some indication that I'm on the right track here?'

'Right *track*?' he said slowly then moved convulsively. 'If you had any idea how much I want you...'

'Rob, I'm falling apart too because I want you so much.'

He picked her up and carried her forward to the vee berth.

It was all over in a matter of minutes.

'Sorry, sorry, sorry,' he said into her hair as he cradled her shell-shocked body. 'That was unforgivable.'

'No, it wasn't.' She pillowed her head against his shoulder. 'It was magnificent.'

'Caiti,' his lips curved, 'thank heavens!'

'I heard wonderful music, Rob,' she said.

'You hear music, but canons and rockets occur to me.'

She considered. 'Perhaps. But there is something about my music I hear. It is fast, enchanting, breathlessly exciting and triumphal at the same time.'

'Triumphal?' He raised his head to look into her eyes. 'Was that how it felt? Or how I felt?'

'You didn't realise it?'

He grimaced.

'Oh, I'm not complaining although it's a miracle I can talk.'

He studied her, the lovely disarray of her hair, the sheen of her skin and some marks he'd made on it. And the expression in her eyes that was faintly teasing but something else as well...

What will be will be? he wondered. Was that what he could see in her eyes, an acceptance that fate had brought them back together and all she could do was go with the flow? Or…what? he wondered. A determination to take their reunion—lightly?

And it occurred to him that there was something eternally mysterious about her. Just when you thought you knew her through and through, she surprised you. So that now, despite accepting his uncontrollable desire for her and being transported by it, he still didn't know whether he would be able to hold her, whether she would be willing to be held if he didn't present her with a good enough case for it.

He caught himself on his next thought—*we'll see about that*—although he knew he meant it, but how to find the words to tell her why he was the way he was? Or, perhaps more importantly, how to change himself?

She didn't allow him to explain anything. She watched the rippling reflections on the cabin ceiling dreamily, then fell asleep, suddenly and completely like a child, in his arms.

After a few minutes, he eased himself away from her, drew the coverlet over her and had a quick shower. Then he went to deal with the fish she'd caught. But as he cleaned and filleted it, his thoughts were still on Caiti Galloway and the enigma she had become.

No, that wasn't true, he reflected. She'd always been an enigma. A virgin when he'd confidently expected her to be experienced. A twenty-one-year-old who'd fallen in love with him so completely—why had he let that happen?—that the shock of discovering there might be more behind his offer of marriage had been catastrophic for her...

He consigned some fish fillets to the ice slurry and reached for the knife sharpener. When the fish was finished and the mess cleared up, he stretched and yawned. And could think of nothing nicer than crawling back into the vee berth beside his wife... He set his teeth suddenly, stared out over the water lilies for a long moment, then did just that.

She didn't stir as he gathered her close again and inhaled the perfume of her skin and the scent of their union. Or stir as he combed the swathe of her hair gently with his fingers—and he accepted the fact that he'd never been moved so much by a woman. Surely that must mean something to her?

It was late afternoon when they stirred again.

Caiti moved in his arms and he opened his eyes to see that her lavender eyes were laughing at him.

'What?' He propped his head on his arm and drew his hand down her body.

She regarded the spikes of his hair sticking up through his fingers and the blue shadows on his jaw. 'I was just thinking—is this what I think it is?'

'What do you think it is?'

'One serious dereliction of duty, I believe. You did invite me for lunch, Mr Leicester.'

'Let me guess—you're starving?'

'I am,' she agreed seriously. 'And, from memory, with cause.'

He frowned faintly. 'I did give you breakfast.'

'I'm talking about a main course that came rather like a bolt from the blue—and with no appetiser.' She pushed back the covers and sat up. And she started to trace little circles in the rough mat of hair on his chest with her fingertip. Then her hand moved lower.

He moved suddenly then pushed himself up against the pillows. 'I think I get your drift.' He closed his hands around her waist and lifted her astride him, bending his knees at the same time.

Caiti leant back against them and trailed her fingers down his diaphragm. 'I always used to feel on top of the world like this.'

'I remember—all too well,' he said rather drily.

She opened her eyes at him. 'Didn't you like it?'

'Oh, I liked it, when I wasn't dying from it.' He cupped her breasts and gently squeezed her nipples through his fingers.

She wriggled her bottom and leant forward so her hair trailed across him. The movement caused the water to slap the outside of the hull.

'I know what you mean,' she said gravely then smiled mischievously. 'Talk about rocking the boat!'

His fingers tightened on her breasts. 'Talking about what might be termed a vessel but is definitely not a boat—things are rising.'

'That's fine with me,' she assured him.

He groaned and pulled her down to him. 'You're a witch, you know,' he growled against her mouth.

'Heaven forbid,' she whispered as she accepted his hard thrust into her body serenely and began to move on him with a lovely, rhythmic grace that Rob Leicester seriously thought he might die from.

The sun was setting when they emerged, showered, dressed and holding hands.

'Hungry?' he queried then added with a wicked grin, 'For food, I mean?'

She smiled dreamily. 'Ravenous. And thirsty.'

'You sit down.' He pointed to a deckchair. 'I'll do the honours.'

First of all he brought her a tall glass of mineral water then a glass of wine. Then he unpacked the portable fridge that ran off the boat batteries, and laid out a feast.

There was mud crab still in the shell but already cracked and a tangy sauce to dip it in. There were cold chicken legs, halved avocados filled with seafood and a ham, mango and pawpaw salad topped with coconut cream lightly dusted with cayenne pepper. For dessert there were strawberries dipped in chocolate.

'Glory be,' Caiti enthused. 'Talk about putting on the Ritz!'

'I did order the best,' he said immodestly, and handed her a plate of crab. 'Mind you, if I'd known you were going to catch the best damn fish caught in these parts for years, I might have cooked myself.'

'Oh! I'd forgotten about that. Really?'

'Really. Forgotten?' He looked across at her quizzically.

She picked up a crab claw, forked a piece of meat out of it and dipped it into the sauce with her fingers. 'Some things can make you forget anything.'

'Some things can,' he agreed. 'Like to stay out for the night?'

Her eyes widened. 'Is it possible?'

He shrugged then looked amused. 'Should be. I get the feeling Clint is a man on a mission.'

'A mission?'

'A mission to reunite us.' He paused and watched her rather intently.

Her hands went still and she stared down at her plate.

'Is that not what you have in mind, Caiti?' he asked at length.

She lifted her gaze to his at last and it was serious but oddly tranquil. 'I had in mind to take each day as it comes for the time being, Rob, that's all.'

He opened his mouth then crushed the retort that had risen to his lips—*how the hell can you say that when you've just slept with me like no other woman ever has?*

He said instead, 'I see.' And marvelled at his lack of originality.

'But I'd love to stay out for the night,' she added.

And now I see what I see, it crossed his mind. A much more cautious Caiti Galloway. Then again, did I really expect that all I had to do was get her back into my bed?

The answer that came to him shook him—yes, he had.

And that made him pose himself another question. Was he still ducking the emotional issues? Still reluctant to dig back through all the turmoil of his life? It seemed so. Or was there a residual fear in him that he couldn't change? If only he could find a way to tear down the barriers permanently, he thought savagely…

'OK. But I'll just check in with Clint on the radio to let him know.'

He got up and turned on the VHF radio and said into the mike, 'Camp Ondine, Camp Ondine, this is Launch Two, Launch Two—do you read me, Clint?'

A burst of static came over the airwaves then Clint's voice, 'Launch Two, Ondine—Rob, thank heavens you called in. Miranda's gone missing!'

Caiti froze.

The trip back to the camp was fast and mostly silent.

As soon as Rob had finished talking to Clint, he'd taken her into his arms and apologised almost desperately.

'Don't,' she said shakily. 'Of course it can't be helped.'

He held her away. 'I know that but…' He stopped and looked at her so frustratedly she was silenced.

But almost immediately he was pulling up the anchor and getting them underway.

Lex was waiting for them on the jetty, looking wild and tearful. She caught the line Caiti threw her then simply laid it down on the jetty and started talking immediately. 'I swear it was only a few minutes that she wasn't under supervision. And now it's dark—'

'Lex,' Rob interrupted, 'just tie us off. Listen,' he turned back to Caiti and lowered his voice, 'can you take care of Lex? She mightn't be much help like this.'

'Of course.'

'Your father is furious, Rob,' Lex gabbled on. 'Furious with me, and it was all going so well, but—'

'What's new?' Rob said coolly.

'The whole camp is searching,' Lex went on. 'I just came down to the jetty in case she'd thought to come and wait for you and Caiti to come back.'

Rob swore then took hold. 'All right. Actually that's not a bad idea. Why don't you and Caiti search the banks around here?' He pulled a powerful torch out of its holder on the cabin wall then opened a hatch and took out a life jacket, which he handed to Caiti. 'It's got a whistle on it. Give it three blasts if you find her.'

He jumped off the boat then leant in over the side and kissed her briefly. 'You take care too.'

*   *   *

It was a few desperate hours before Miranda was found unharmed in a rocky gully half a mile from the camp but deeply scared by her plight.

It was Rob who found her and relayed the news through a two-way radio.

By this time, Caiti had met Frank Leicester in highly difficult circumstances. He'd greeted her with the utmost suspicion and barked at her, 'Well, well, the runaway bride! What have you got to say for yourself?'

'What has that got to do with anything, Frank?' Lex demanded tearfully.

He was tough and leathery with grey hair but a fine figure of a man, Rob's father. You could also see the almost intolerable strain in his eyes, and it prompted Caiti not to respond in kind.

She merely said, 'How do you do? Yes, I'm Caiti Galloway.'

That was when the call came through, and half an hour later Rob appeared with Miranda wrapped in a blanket in his arms.

The reunion between mother, father and daughter was ecstatic as Rob handed her over and stood by, watching, with an inscrutable expression.

Then Lex turned to thank him, and his father looked up at last. 'Son, I can't thank you enough.' He put out his hand.

Rob shook it. 'May I make a suggestion? Take care of them *both*; they're pretty special.'

Frank put his arm around Lex and his hand in Miranda's. 'I intend to,' he said fervently, and he led his wife and his daughter away.

Caiti turned away to deal with some tears. When she turned back, Rob had disappeared. And a phrase sprang into Caiti's mind from nowhere—*the odd man out*. Had he always been the odd one out?

Her heart beat so painfully for him, she flinched. But before she went to find him, she visited her cabin briefly then collected a couple of stiff brandies from the bar.

He was on the beach, in the same spot she'd left him all those months ago, sitting on a bench.

He hadn't changed, he was grazed and dusty, his shirt was torn and his jeans were streaked with dirt. And it wasn't until she moved into his line of sight that he became aware of her presence.

'Hi,' she said and handed over a glass. 'My turn to be the restorer.'

'Thanks.' He looked down at it. 'Miranda saw a wallaby and decided to follow it.'

'She might be one of those kids that needs some sort of a tracking device—perhaps a transmitting bracelet?'

His lips twisted then he sipped his drink. 'I was beginning to think—all sorts of things.'

'I know. We all were. Rob,' she took a breath and sat down beside him, 'I—'

But he forestalled her. 'All sorts of things and not

only about Miranda. Caiti,' he said with an intensity that surprised her, 'can you ever forgive me for being such a—a coward and a fool?'

Her eyes widened. 'I don't understand.'

'Neither did I—well, not completely, but for a long time now I've felt *displaced* yet I couldn't bring myself to admit it to anyone else. Even this afternoon on the boat I wasn't sure if I could bear to dig deep enough to explain it to you.'

She held her breath for a moment then forced herself to relax.

He went on after a moment, 'But something about thinking we'd lost Miranda, then their joy in each other, really made me see what I was doing to myself—and you.'

'Go on,' she whispered, with a spring of hope welling in her heart. She'd been going to tell him that the same sequence of events had helped her to understand him more, but how much better for it to come from him?

'My father,' he said and stared seaward for a long moment, then dropped his gaze to his drink, 'well, for a long time he didn't believe I was his son, nor was my mother too sure.'

'How did that happen?' she asked quietly.

'The usual way.' He grimaced. 'Their marriage got on the rocks and my mother had an affair but she came back to him. Then I happened along, slightly premature or—not his son. They battled on until I was six or seven then they separated, but even at that age I knew—' he gestured '—I knew I could never measure up to Steve in my father's eyes, and, even if I didn't understand what all the disagreement was about, I realised that somehow I was the cause of it.'

Caiti closed her eyes and wondered how anyone could do that to a child.

'To complicate matters, Steve is the living image of Dad, but if I take after anyone it's my mother's side of the family.'

'What happened to your mother?'

'After the divorce, some time after it, she remarried and now lives in Perth. I spent eight years with her, away from Leicester Downs, and that's where I picked up my interest in this kind of thing.' He waved a hand. 'Her family owned a chain of country hotels.'

'That explains it!' Caiti smiled at him. 'So, why did you go back?'

'I couldn't stand the man she married.' He grimaced. 'By then I was fifteen and old enough to take issue with whose damn son I really was. Heaven alone knows why they hadn't done it earlier except, I suppose, until DNA was common practice, you could prove who your father wasn't but not necessarily who he was.'

'But you were his son after all—did he welcome you back?' Caiti asked.

'He tried his hardest but there was a lot of water under the bridge by then, and he and Steve were very close. Still, I discovered I was happy to be back with them until…' He stopped.

'Stella?' she suggested.

'Stella,' he repeated then added softly, 'Talk about someone who traded on her looks, her body and her charm, she was the ultimate example of it.'

Caiti shivered involuntarily. 'I see.'

He put his arm around her. 'Do you, though? Yes, she made my life hell for a while. I was actually at university when I met her and living away from home. Then I took her out to the station for a long weekend, where, unbeknownst to me, she summed up the situation pretty accurately. Steve was the older son, possibly the favoured son and most likely to inherit the bulk of it. That's when she dumped me for him.'

'And Steve had no qualms about it?'

'Steve,' Rob broke off and sighed, 'never had a chance. All he'd ever wanted to do was run Leicester Downs; he's a fair dinkum cattle man. I'm not saying he's a country bumpkin, far from it, but women hadn't featured greatly in his life and she…she just bowled him over.'

'But it must have made things so awkward.'

He rubbed his fingers down her arm. 'I still had another two years of my degree to do so it wasn't hard to stay away as much as possible. Of course, the time came when I had to go back, but by then they'd been married for over a year. They also had their own house, their own life to a certain extent and Dad had taken over another pastoral lease that I went back to run.'

'So you felt there was enough separation for it not to be a problem?'

He looked out over the sea. 'I suppose so. Nor had I, until then, any reason to believe that Stella hadn't genuinely fallen for Steve. I soon discovered otherwise and that's when I knew I had to get away and came up with this idea. That is also, Caiti, when I stopped loving Stella and saw her for the devious person she really is.'

He paused. 'The thing was, though, it may have been the only way to go but once again I was on the outside—displaced again, you could say—and that was much more of a blow than anything Stella had ever meant to me.'

'When did Lex come on the scene?'

'Round about the same time.'

Caiti flinched inwardly.

'Anyway,' he went on, 'this time I decided—that was it! They could all play happy families or *unhappy* families to their hearts' content but I'd concentrate on building my empire.'

'Oh, Rob,' she said softly. 'That's when you built a wall around you.'

He drew her closer. 'In hindsight, yes. Mind you, I never dreamt they would extend beyond the family or that I'd be infected with such an intense level of wariness about love and marriage.'

'It's a miracle you're not more cynical than you are,' she said then bit her lip.

But he smiled ruefully. 'As you say. Then Steve had his accident, and do you know what happened?' He shook his head as if it still amazed him. 'It hit me out of the blue that to go back and run Leicester Downs would be the one thing I needed to do to prove once and for all to my father that I was a worthy son, despite all this.' He gestured again to take in Camp Ondine and his other achievements. 'Strange, isn't it?'

'To feel that way about a father who had virtually disowned you?'

He put his glass down and rubbed his jaw reflectively. 'There are times when I have to blame my mother more than my father. She was the one who was unfaithful then couldn't be sure whose child she was carrying. She was—' he stopped and sighed '—*they* were such a volatile, explosive mix of love and hate—'

'You know what I think?' she broke in. 'Sometimes it happens that way between two people and they're powerless to change it or change the fallout. But she is your mother and he is your father, nothing can change that.'

'Perhaps,' he conceded. 'Anyway, for whatever reason, I got a very powerful inner call to go back and take over Leicester Downs but...' He stopped.

'And here's where it gets interesting,' she said huskily. 'There was a complication in the form of me.'

'Caiti,' he shook his head, 'I'll never forgive my-self for what I said to Lex that day over the phone but I was just so…frustrated because Dad had turned my offer down only hours earlier.'

She gasped. 'I didn't know that. Why?'

'Strangely enough—over you. He assumed I'd married you for all the wrong reasons. He was ex-tremely angry.'

Caiti blinked as she remembered the other thing Lex had said on the phone that fateful day about his father being furious…

Rob went on, 'He accused me of marrying the first girl I could lay my hands on, which could only add more complications to an already complicated situ-ation. I tried to explain but he wouldn't listen. That's when Lex intervened—on the phone. That's when I was goaded into stripping it all down to the bare essentials in a—I don't know,' he frowned, 'in a rather bloody-minded *since that's what you all think of me, what the hell was I supposed to do?* mood.'

'But why would your father automatically have assumed that?' Caiti queried.

He heaved a sigh. 'Stella wasn't particularly dis-creet but, in the strange way these things often work out, Steve didn't know—or appeared not to, any-way—what was going on. Dad was another matter though and he extracted a promise from me that I wasn't doing anything to harm their marriage. Perhaps you can imagine how I felt?'

She nodded.

'So I not only told him she was quite safe from me but also that I would never go back to Leicester Downs without a wife of my own.'

Caiti drew an unsteady breath.

'I know,' he said barely audibly, 'all the evidence is piling up against me well and truly.'

She was silent.

He got up and prowled down to the water's edge.

Eighteen months ago it had been wild and windy with the tang of salt on the air. Tonight it was calm and a pale new moon was sailing across the star-laden heavens.

Caiti waited until he came back to stand in front of her. 'I guess that brings us to—you and me?' she said a little shakily.

'It does,' he agreed. 'And the fact that, although I wasn't prepared to admit I'd fallen in love with you, I couldn't let you go.'

She looked up into his eyes. 'But you still can't say it, Rob, although now perhaps I can understand why.'

'Yes, I can, Caiti. I loved you then, I love you now and I always will. Unfortunately, and I only have myself to blame, when you left me I...erected a few more walls, and when you came back looking for a divorce, if anything, I reinforced them.'

She took a distressed little breath. 'I guess...well, I guess that's understandable and partly my fault.'

'Understandable?' He smiled but with no amusement. 'It now looks like insanity to me. I couldn't bear the thought of losing you again, I couldn't bear the thought of you with another man, but I still couldn't...' He shrugged.

She blinked confusedly. 'You were furious—more furious when you discovered there *was* no other man.'

'Because of what—talk about torments of the damned!—I'd gone through, thinking of you with someone else. And because,' he shoved his hands in his pockets, 'you seemed to think it still made sense for us to part.'

'I was working without a script, or only a partial script.'

'I know, but tonight, watching Dad, Lex and Miranda, I suddenly realised what my real problem was.'

She looked a question at him.

'A lack of guts. So,' he shrugged, 'I had a bit of a roller-coaster ride but many people do. To perpetuate it all in the form of holding you at arm's length mentally, though, was—is—now unthinkable. To go on being a disillusioned loner in the face of *your* love and the most wonderful thing that's ever happened to me would be the act of a coward, but not only that, it would also be giving sanction to all that has gone before.'

He paused and searched her eyes. 'I don't know if this means anything to you, Caiti, but not only do

I *love* you, but I also haven't even been able to look at let alone touch another woman since you ran away.'

Her eyes widened and she was transported back in the day to the first time he'd made love to her on the boat. Why it hadn't occurred to her at the time she had no idea, but his lovemaking had had all the hallmarks of a man who had been celibate for a long time.

'That,' he said unevenly, 'is how much you mean to me.'

Tears of joy gathered but she blinked them away. 'It's been the same for me,' she said huskily.

'So?'

The question hung in the air between them.

She got to her feet. 'Rob, there's something you haven't noticed yet but I came to find you to show you that I loved you no matter what was in your past or whether you could talk about it or not.' She held her left hand out to him, palm down.

His gaze dropped to it, and his diamond-studded wedding ring on her ring finger.

'*Caiti?*' Her name tore out of him on an incredulous breath.

'I think it's time we took up our marriage, Rob. Don't you?'

'Sweetheart…' For a moment he seemed helpless beneath the shock of it, then he reached for her and held her as if he'd never let her go.

CHAPTER TEN

'THERE'S one thing I don't understand,' Caiti sat up and said.

They were in the honeymoon suite, much more palatial than either of their cabins.

Whoever had decorated it had really gone to town to create a rainforest theme that was also the height of luxury. The walls and carpet were gum-leaf green. The bed was king-sized with gauzy white hangings and the linen reflected the colours and flowers of Aussie bush icons—lily pink, bottlebrush red, corn yellow.

And, in a glassed-in alcove looking out over the forest, there was a topaz-coloured marble spa bath.

She and Rob were lounging back in it, in drifts of bubbles, sipping champagne with aromatic candles shedding soft light and scenting the air—until Caiti sat up to make her comment.

'What would that be?' he queried as he watched the bubbles slide down her skin and reveal her breasts, all rosy and satiny. And it came to him that, although he had not that long ago made love to her most comprehensively, it mightn't be long before he wanted to do so again...

'You said your father refused your offer to go back and run the station, but you did go, didn't you?'

'Yep.'

'What made him change his mind?'

'I got—' a faint smile tugged at his lips '—and you should appreciate this, Caiti, but I got quite mean and nasty.'

'Oh! How so?'

'I laid down the law. I told him there was no fool like an old fool, there was no way he could cope on his own and I was sick to death of the way he persisted in mucking up my life. I told him it was all thanks to him, even if indirectly, that you had run away but I wouldn't rest until I got you back. And in the meantime he would just have to make the best of it because I was taking up the reins.'

Caiti shivered.

He drew her back into his arms. 'I know, it wasn't pleasant, but in the end it worked. We came to a much better understanding of each other and I think some new ideas I had really appealed to him. Look, he'll always be difficult, he's that kind of man, but I guess I've made my peace with him.'

'I'm so happy for you,' she murmured. 'How…how are Steve and Stella going?'

He nuzzled the top of her head and grinned. 'You do like all the ends tied up, don't you?'

'I could be that kind of person,' she agreed gravely.

'Steve was in and out of hospital and convalescent

care in Cairns for nearly a year. Stella moved down to be with him. I don't know if it was the shock of nearly losing him, but she seems to be much more contented. May we talk about us for a change?'

'Certainly. What did you have in mind?'

He settled them comfortably side by side. 'Plans for the future. Where you would like to live and all the things we neglected to discuss last time around.'

Caiti smiled dreamily. 'Don't they say home is where the heart is? Well, mine's with you.'

He took some time to kiss her. Then, 'All the same, we can't spend the rest of our lives in guest cabins, so I had a thought, subject to your approval. Since Ondine's my headquarters, should we build our own home here?'

She sat up again. 'Rob, I would love that!'

'You remind me of a jack-in-the-box,' he said wryly. 'How come you're so full of energy?'

'I've never felt better in my life!'

He groaned. 'Just as well I also had in mind to suggest a job. Or, more accurately, a partnership.'

She hesitated. 'You don't have to do that.'

He sat up himself. 'Yes, I do. I need you, Caiti.'

'How? Why?'

'You may not realise this, but when you're around, the place seems to be much more alive, the guests seem to be much more—I don't know—involved.'

She stared into his eyes. 'Really?'

'Yes,' he kissed her forehead, 'really. Not that I expect you to work yourself to the bone, but if you would like to be in charge of guest entertainment I couldn't think of anyone more perfect for it.'

'Funnily enough, I had some thoughts along those lines myself, once,' she said slowly.

He looked at her closely.

Caiti chewed her lip for a moment. 'It's struck me at times that this would be a marvellous backdrop for some culture.'

'Go on.'

'Perhaps an annual musical event? Maybe a writer's workshop conducted by a popular author? An art fair, say, and not only painting but there's also some wonderful weaving, pottery and ceramics done in this area. How about a gourmet-cooking course? How about a celebration of Aboriginal culture and music? How—?'

'Stop,' he said softly and combed his fingers through the rough silk of her hair.

'You don't like the idea.'

'I love it. You're a genius.'

They lay back together, Caiti lost for words for once as the future unfolded before her.

Then she was struck by a thought. 'If only Marion could know how things have turned out…' She stopped and put her hands to her mouth. 'Marion! I forgot! She was on my mind all morning then…' She gestured helplessly.

'Caiti,' his gaze softened, 'you did all you could.'

'But she'll be—'

'She sounded relieved. She said she hadn't realised

how she'd got into the habit of being a doormat. And while her life looks a bit bleak, it's also as if a weight has lifted off her. She sent you a message, by the way, that I—uh—saw fit not to pass on.'

Caiti's eyes widened. 'You did?'

He sipped some champagne. 'Being slightly demented, yes.'

'What was it?' She frowned.

He ran his fingers through his damp hair. 'She said, tell Caiti she was an inspiration.'

'I was? How?'

'In the way you stood up for yourself and refused to be a convenient wife.'

Caiti shivered and he put his glass down to sit up abruptly and pulled her into his arms. 'That's over, my darling.'

'I know. But I can't help being sad for her—and feeling there's a twisted kind of irony to it all. I was pulling out all the stops to get her to the altar, not the opposite.'

'Then this may help. Derek also called me. He's gone after her. He's had the shock of his life and he desperately doesn't want to lose her. Although the wedding has been cancelled.'

Caiti relaxed slightly. 'I suppose—what will be will be.'

'Yes. Uh—talking about sex…'

'Were we?' she asked innocently then relented at his expression. 'It was glorious,' she told him seriously.

'It was also a record. Three times in one day.'

'Pretty impressive,' she agreed. 'Were you thinking of…setting an even higher one?'

He scanned her face, to see only grave interest in her eyes. 'Well…no.'

'Because you feel that four times in one day might be indicative of some form of excessive behaviour?' she queried with academic precision.

He narrowed his eyes. 'Do you?'

She considered the matter. 'I don't know. But I do happen to be in possession of some knowledge that tells me you're worrying needlessly.'

'Such as?' He frowned.

'There's a clock on the wall over there.' She pointed.

He squinted over his shoulder. 'Never noticed it. Hell, it's two-thirty in the morning!'

She agreed that it was. 'That takes us into the next day, so I feel we'd be quite safe.'

He turned back to her, his eyes alight with laughter. 'So be it, then.'

'Would you like to have an event of some kind to celebrate this *turn* of events?' Rob asked.

They were still in the honeymoon suite, having slept late. Their breakfast had been delivered to them and they were now enjoying their coffee.

Caiti looked at him askance over the rim of her cup. 'You're not talking weddings, are you, by any chance?'

He was dressed in fresh khakis, and had just spoken to Clint by phone while she'd showered; she wore only her silk wrap.

'Definitely not! We've had one of those and I'll probably be allergic to anyone else's for a long time to come. What about a safari and a christening?'

She put her cup down and blinked at him. 'We haven't had a baby yet.'

His gaze lingered on her curves beneath the colourful silk in a way that made her heart-beat trip, then slid his hand across the table to cover hers. 'At this rate that might be sooner than we think. But no, I was thinking of christening Camp Caiti with your parents and my father and Lex in attendance.'

Caiti sat up excitedly then slumped. 'My father's in Patagonia.'

'As a matter fact, he's here.'

'What?'

'He and your mother arrived this morning, looking for you. I haven't seen them yet; Clint passed on the news. They registered as Mr and Mrs Galloway, like a normal married couple, and took one cabin.'

'I don't believe it,' Caiti said stupidly, then she sprang up. 'Rob! They must be back together again!'

'It looks like it. That's three reunions now. Your parents, Lex and Dad, you and I. All we need is for Derek to work some magic with Marion and this whole screwy period will be reversed. Come here.'

Caiti sat down on his lap, laughing helplessly.

'So what do you think?' he queried as he nuzzled her neck. 'Good idea or not?'

She laid her palm on his cheek. 'Can Camp Caiti cope?'

'It's finally finished. I decided to put in some refinements so I could take you there in a bit of comfort.'

'Thank you,' she said softly. 'That would be a perfect way for them to get to know each other, and us to get to know them. I'll look forward to it!'

He kissed her then set her on her feet reluctantly. 'They'll be dying to see you.'

Caiti threw off her robe and waltzed across the room.

'Now, that,' he drawled, 'is really something to look forward to.'

Caiti stopped and turned back to him with her eyebrows raised.

He got up and came towards her but didn't touch her. Instead, his gaze travelled from the sweep of her loose hair lying on one shoulder down her naked body. 'To be able to see you like this for the rest of my life,' he said barely audibly.

She stood on her toes, put her hands on his shoulders and, with love shining in her eyes, replied simply, 'It's my pleasure.'

SILHOUETTE Romance

From first love to forever, these love stories
are fairy tale romances for today's woman.

Silhouette Desire

Modern, passionate reads that are powerful and provocative.

Silhouette SPECIAL EDITION™

Emotional, compelling stories that capture the intensity
of living, loving and creating a family in today's world.

Silhouette INTIMATE MOMENTS™

A roller-coaster read that delivers romantic thrills
in a world of suspense, adventure and more.

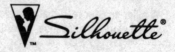

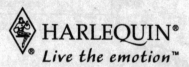

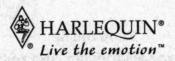